To Bryan &
Mary

Love,

Dale

HARDIN'S LEGACY

HARDIN'S LEGACY

---~---

Endeavor to Do Right

a novel

R. Dale Bunch

iUniverse, Inc.
New York Bloomington Shanghai

HARDIN'S LEGACY
Endeavor to Do Right

Copyright © 2008 by R. Dale Bunch

All rights reserved. No part of this book may be used or reproduced by any means, graphic, electronic, or mechanical, including photocopying, recording, taping or by any information storage retrieval system without the written permission of the publisher except in the case of brief quotations embodied in critical articles and reviews.

iUniverse books may be ordered through booksellers or by contacting:

iUniverse
1663 Liberty Drive
Bloomington, IN 47403
www.iuniverse.com
1-800-Authors (1-800-288-4677)

Because of the dynamic nature of the Internet, any Web addresses or links contained in this book may have changed since publication and may no longer be valid.

ISBN: 978-0-595-48347-1 (pbk)
ISBN: 978-0-595-71816-0 (cloth)
ISBN: 978-0-595-60437-1 (ebk)

Printed in the United States of America

Certain characters in this work are historical figures, and certain events portrayed did take place. However, this is a work of fiction. All of the other characters, names, and events as well as all places, incidents, organizations, and dialogue in this novel are either the products of the author's imagination or are used fictitiously.

Content Editor: Meredith Bunch

Designer/Illustrator: Garrick Reid

All poems contained in Hardin's Legacy except "Lasca," the Texas folklore poem, were written by the author.

For Bev

Contents

Preface xiii

Lone Jack 1

John Robert 4

The Federals 6

Leaving Home. 10

The South Grand 12

A New Home 18

After the War 22

Young Hardin 24

Finding the Road 26

Growing Up 29

Birthday Present 32

Time To Go 35

Traveling to Quincy 39

Trouble on the Road. 43

Moving On. 47

Crossing the River. 50

New Friends 53

Lillie	57
Quincy	59
The Dinner Date	64
Falling Ill	67
Going Home	70
Reunion with Friends	73
Building a Future	75
Directions in Life	79
Reuniting with Lillie	82
Taking the Risk	84
J. Belt	86
The Farm	89
The Slagle Boys	92
Changing Times	95
Joyous Love	99
New Life on the Farm	102
Adjusting to Farming	106
The Hot Summer	109
The Quest for Satisfaction	115
Growing Responsibilities	117
Losing Lillie	119
The Pain of Loss	121
Minnie Etta Slavens	124
Coping with Life Alone	126
Hardin's Renewal	128

A Difficult Romance	130
A Picnic with Minnie	132
A Summer of Floods	136
A New Life	139
Renewal and Discovery	142
Life's Mystery	145
Good-bye, Beloved Hardin	148
Resolution of Respect	152
Minnie	153
The Slavens Family	157
Life Without Hardin	160
The Slavens Lend a Hand	163
Hardin's Children Grow Up	166
Minnie's Decision	169
J. Belt Hammond	171
Changing Times	173
Losing Everything	175
Minnie's Final Years	177
References	181

Preface

I began thinking about my ancestors a few years ago and wondering what their lives were like. What sort of impact did they have upon my life?

When I dug into old records and histories, I came to realize that my grandfather, Hardin Rogers Hammond, led an interesting and fruitful life. He was one of the founders of my family, and by studying the scraps of information I could find, I learned a great deal about the strong values and philosophies in which he believed. I believe wholeheartedly that his strong values are also evident in the lives of the following generations.

We are about to go back in time and trace the footsteps of my grandfather, Hardin Hammond, and his family. We will see how he persevered and prospered until he met with a terrible tragedy that changed my family's future forever.

The names and dates in *Hardin's Legacy* are accurate, as far as I know. I pieced them together from our family's small amount of written history and information that is available today. Many of the stories in this book are true; they were either written down or passed along to me by word of mouth. I have carefully woven these facts about Hardin and his family together with plausible fiction and a spirit of love and respect for my ancestors.

Lone Jack

A giant Blackjack oak tree stood high on a hill overlooking the prairie in Jackson County, Missouri. This large tree served as a landmark that guided pioneers as they traveled back and forth across the land. Over time, the town of Lone Jack grew on that hill and was named for the Blackjack oak tree that marked its beginning.

Settlers who were crossing the country often stopped at Lone Jack for rest and supplies. Because it was blessed with a good supply of water and trees, many chose Lone Jack for their homes. The area's population steadily grew, and though it soon became a town, it remained quiet and peaceful. Stores, churches, and businesses provided useful services to families living within traveling distance. Lone Jack was a friendly country community that provided a good life for its citizens.

On August 15–16, 1862, the Civil War erupted with full force upon the people of Lone Jack. During those two extremely hot August days, the town was caught in one of the fiercest battles between the North and South that would ever be fought in Missouri. John Robert Hammond and his wife, Mary Owen Hammond—my great grandparents—and their three small children listened to the far-away sounds of the battle that took place on August 16.

"What will we do, John?" Mary asked. Her fear for herself and her family was growing as the war came closer and closer to their country home.

John Robert stood quietly in the front yard. Mary saw the tension in his tanned face and blue eyes. He was fully alert, his mind racing and searching for a solution to their plight. His right ear was turned in the direction of the sounds as he tried to predict the war's outcome.

"If the Confederates win, we'll be okay for the time being. If the Federals win at Lone Jack, I think it would be best if we headed deeper into Missouri. I have hope that we can find a safe place to live until the outcome of the war is decided.

When the war is over, we can come back home. But right now there are too many Federals; the Confederates can't hold them off for very long."

Looking down at his boots, John Robert felt desperation as he sought a plan to save his family and himself. Soon, the outcome of the battle at Lone Jack would become clear. He needed to be prepared for the consequences and be ready to fight if he had to. But he was a schoolteacher, and fighting was the last thing that he wanted to do.

During the terrible fighting, the Confederates defended the town of Lone Jack from the determined aggressors. The Federals used two sixteen-pound cannons as their most powerful weapons. The cannons fired one after the other, forcing the Confederates behind their barricades.

The Federals fired their cannons as fast as they could, ramming home and discharging the canisters at the defending Confederates. Each time the cannons fired, dozens of iron balls flew into the main street of town and rained upon the Confederates. The smoke from the cannons, small arms, and other weapons soon formed a cloud across the battle zone that neither side could see through.

Focusing upon the two cannons, the Confederates fired all of their guns at the Federal battery. To cover their position, the Federals brought their horses up front so they could protect the soldiers with their bodies. The Confederates continued to fire at the frightened animals, and one Federal company alone lost twenty-six horses. The screams and awful groans of those dying horses echoed throughout the town as they fell into a dreadful pile in front of the Federals.

The battle went back and forth. When the Confederates finally captured the guns, the Federal Army regrouped and recaptured them. Finally, the Confederates began to retreat, but Colonel Coffee suddenly broke out of the woods north of the town with more than eight hundred fresh Confederate soldiers and made ready for battle. His appearance refreshed the Confederates' morale and presented the Federals with overwhelming odds.

The captain of the Federal forces realized that his chances of winning the battle that day were shrinking at a rapid rate. The troops were worn out, supplies were low, and the ammunition was almost gone. Realizing his army's desperate plight and trying to save as many soldiers as he could, the Federal captain ordered his army to retreat and head back to Lexington. Most of his officers were either dead or wounded. They couldn't take the wounded with them, so they left them near the burned ruins of the Cave Hotel, where they would either be killed or cared for by the rebels. Federal dead were scattered all over the battlefield, left where they had fallen as a testimony to the dreadful fight.

The town of Lone Jack was a sorrowful sight. Thirteen homes and businesses were completely destroyed. Throughout the town, two hundred men lay dead, dying, or wounded in the streets and buildings. Because some of those who had died were just boys from the community, the citizens were heartbroken over the battle. Those boys had only recently joined the army due to the recruiters who had come to Lone Jack.

The worst death of all was that of a young mother, Lucinda Cave. Lucinda and her husband, Bart, owned the Cave Hotel. The Federal Army had commandeered the hotel for its own use the night before the fight. When they set the hotel on fire, Lucinda and her family were forced to make a run for different cover. As she ran across a field, Lucinda was shot by a stray bullet. She managed to tend to her children out in the field while she was still wounded. Within a month, young Lucinda was dead. She was buried in the cemetery east of town. Lucinda had been one of the town's most beloved citizens, and everyone mourned the loss of her cheerful and helpful presence in their community.

1862

Men fought and died that awful year,
Each joined the army to be a man.
The terrible fighting showed their fear,
The ones that lived just ran.

Young boys lay dead and dying,
You had to look away.
Finally the smoke and cries had cleared,
But there was nothing left to say.

John Robert

On that hot, August evening, the occasional rustle of squirrels taking their supper of hickory nuts in the trees broke the silence of the stilled leaves. It was quiet, and yet John Robert Hammond had a strange foreboding—a feeling that everything was not as peaceful as it might seem.

Waiting to decide what to do was wearing John Robert down. If the Confederates couldn't beat back the Federal soldiers, then his home and his family's way of life would be lost. The war would change everything.

John Robert and Mary Owen lived in Cass County, Missouri. The county was on the Kansas border in western Missouri. All but a few of its residents sympathized with the Confederate cause. Across the border in Kansas, the Federals had been building forts and amassing troops, planning to push westward into Missouri. John and Mary had spent their adult lives teaching school and raising their three small children. They didn't believe in the war, and they wished to continue their lives as they were. Unfortunately, the war was now coming to them.

Early the next morning, several men rode up to the Hammond farm to talk with John Robert. It was August 17, 1862, and the Battle of Lone Jack was over. The Confederates had finally driven the Federals out of town, but the cost had been high. The men needed John Robert's help to bury the dead in Lone Jack.

John Robert saddled up his horse. He told Mary Owen that he would be back that night. The men rode off in a cloud of dry, August dust, dreading what they would find when they arrived at the scene of the battle. They felt that it was their duty to do what they could for the remaining citizens of Lone Jack.

When they arrived in Lone Jack, the men choked back their tears and sorrow at the terrible sight of the battle's aftermath. They learned that 147 Federals lay dead or wounded, scattered throughout the town. Forty-seven Confederates also needed burial, but many more had been taken away by relatives to be buried at home. On Main Street, between seventy-five and a hundred horses lay dead or dying. The men braced themselves for the gruesome task that had to be done.

The blistering, August sun made it imperative that the bodies of the dead be buried quickly. They dug two long, parallel trenches in the shade of the large Blackjack tree. Then they separated the bodies according to whether they were friends or foes. John Robert walked along the trenches, surveying the bodies as they awaited a covering of earth. There were a total of 119 deceased Federals, and they were laid two bodies across down the long trench to utilize as much of the space as possible. All the Federals were buried together in that one trench.

The other trench contained the bodies of the forty-seven Confederates who had fought so valiantly to defend their town. They were laid in the ground in the same manner. John Robert and the others shoveled dirt back into the trenches over the bodies. They worked through the hot afternoon, covering the men who had fought so bravely. They spoke few words, and each man thought about the tragedy of the lives that were no more.

A local farmer, Tom Roupe, was assigned the grisly task of removing the pile of dead horses from the town. Tom recruited some men, and together they removed the saddles and harnesses from the dead horses. Then they pulled the animals' bodies out of town with a team of live horses and piled them in a heap. They chose an area away from town so the citizens wouldn't have to deal with the sight and smell of the dead horses. Over time, buzzards, coyotes, foxes, and other animals would reduce the dead horses to a large pile of bones. The sight of those bones would serve as a reminder of the terrible battle for many years to come.

The work took the men all day. They were all tired and heartbroken by the time they left Lone Jack for their homes. As they rode through the evening, each man wondered in his own way why this terrible war had to happen.

Echo

The echo of the sounds of war
Came from far away.
John Robert knew that bloody gore
Was ruining Lone Jack that day.

A teacher and a scholar too,
His family crowded round.
He didn't know what to do.
For now, he'd stand his ground.

The Federals

At Lone Jack, the Confederate rebels who were left knew that their position was untenable. The Federals would soon return with larger forces. The rebels' only hope was to pack up their families and move farther south into Missouri. They had to leave the seriously wounded with the citizens who were staying and get out of Lone Jack as soon as possible.

It was late at night when John Robert returned home from Lone Jack. He was tired and scared for the lives of his family. He lay awake that night wondering what they should do.

The next morning, Mary Owen sat on the front porch. The children were huddled close around her. She held little baby Hardin in her arms while J. Belt, who was two years old, and Pearlie, who was four years old, stood next to her. Hardin gave out a small cry that told Mary Owen that he was ready for more breast-feeding. At a year old, Hardin was a big baby with a huge appetite. She was pleased that he was so healthy.

After little Willie had died, the other children had been comforts to her. He had been her first baby, but somehow, he had never seemed to have the strength for life. The cold, winter days and nights the previous year had been too much for his frail little body, and when he had gotten the flu, he had quietly left the world of the living while Mary Owen had gently rocked him back and forth in her arms.

Mary Owen and John Robert had drawn closer together that winter as they laid Willie to rest in the Cass County Cemetery. Their hope was that he was in a higher place and that they would join him there someday.

John Robert stood in his front yard in his leather coat to ward off the morning chill. He leaned on the picket fence by the gate as he wondered what he could do to save his family from the dangerous environment they were in. His boots showed the wear of walking back and forth to the schoolhouse where he taught grade school. John Robert was known as a capable and intelligent man and was well respected in their little country community.

Mary Owen rocked back and forth in one of the two rocking chairs on the wide front porch of their attractive home as she fed little Hardin. J. Belt and Pearlie stood close by her, watching Hardin happily sucking away at her nipple. She knew that she was now pregnant with another child. She and John Robert looked forward to expanding their family and raising another little one. It would be several months before this child would be born; she had only recently discovered her pregnancy.

Looking down the dirt road that led up to their house, John Robert could see a faint cloud of dust rising in the distance. Their home in Cass County, Missouri, didn't get many visitors at that time of the morning. John Robert wondered who was riding so hard down the road and why he seemed to be in such a hurry.

John Robert had just been thinking about how he hated what was happening to the country. He had hoped that the war would end soon and that he could keep on teaching school and raising his family in a peaceful way. But after the Battle of Lone Jack, John Robert knew that the war wouldn't end for a long time.

Now the rider was coming into sight. John Robert saw that the horse was lathered from the hard ride. Frothy foam showed white around the black horse's mouth. It was evidence of a frantic ride. The news must be important if it was being delivered with such haste and emotion. The rider's shirt was drenched with sweat. John could now see that the rider was young Billy Johnson. Billy lived with his parents on their farm five miles down the road.

Billy started shouting as soon as he came close. "The Federals are coming! There's a whole army marching right down this road. They took our house and are talking with Mom and Dad right now. They want information. They are taking every house that they come to. We are packing up and leaving for my aunt's house tomorrow morning. They will kill us if we don't go. Dad sent me to warn you. They are coming!"

A sudden feeling of fear and confusion struck John Robert in the pit of his stomach as Billy quickly rode off to warn others down the road. He saw Mary Owen's frightened look as she sat in her chair with the children around her. She had heard Billy and knew that this was a serious situation. John Robert went into the house and collected his guns: a pistol, a shotgun, and a rifle. At the back of the house, he crawled under the flooring in the crawl space until he reached the middle of the area. He hid the guns in a depression in the ground. He knew that whatever happened, he would need to have his guns.

Soon, five soldiers in blue uniforms rode up to the house. A two-horse wagon with a driver rolled along behind them. The men looked tired and dirty, and they all had rifles next to their saddles. John could see that they also had pistols on their belts. One man rode out in front. His stripes and medals showed that he was a Federal officer. His uniform was covered in dust. Bloodshot eyes peered out of the man's tanned, bearded face. He spoke to John Robert briskly.

"We need supplies, and we'll be taking your house. If you move from that spot, you will be shot. We haven't any time right now for funny business."

With their guns trained on John Robert, the men went into the house and began loading all of the meat, lard, other food, harnesses, and whatever else that they could find into the wagon. They took bedclothes and some of John's and Mary's clothes. Little Pearlie grabbed onto the comforter one man was taking. She said, "That's my mom's comforter." The man yanked the blanket out of Pearlie's hands and threw it into the wagon. Pearlie was confused and scared and began to cry.

After they had completed their devilish work, the captain ordered John Robert to pull off his coat. As he pulled it off, John Robert said, "If you need this coat worse than I do, then take it." The captain then ordered John Robert to put the coat on again. That was enough for John Robert! Mad now, he said, "I will put it back on when I'm good and ready!"

The captain put a cocked rifle to John Roberts's breast, and another soldier put a pistol to his head. Just then, Mary Owen handed little Hardin to Pearlie and jumped down off the porch, putting herself between the rifle and John's breast and knocking the pistol aside. The rifle discharged, wounding Mary Owen in the arm. She had saved John Robert. John Robert caught her in his arms and held her. They sat down on the ground together, holding each other tightly.

"You folks have to move. We are taking over this house for our officers. We will be back tomorrow morning. If you are still here when we come back, you will be shot," the officer said tersely.

John Robert's world was changing fast! He wanted his gun. He was angry and wanted to kill this man who was forcing him to leave his home. Even though he knew that the other soldiers would shoot him immediately, he was mad enough to believe that his honor would be worth the sacrifice. But John Robert also knew that he had to protect Mary Owen and the children. He silently swallowed his pride and conceded defeat. It wasn't easy for a proud man like John Robert to back down from a fight.

"I understand," John Robert said. He knew that they would be lucky to escape with their lives.

The soldier turned to the others and said, "Let's ride on down the road. We need more food and houses." The soldiers left with the wagon, which was loaded with the family's food and other goods, and rode off in a cloud of dust without even looking back.

Mary Owen understood her man better than he would ever know. She knew that his impulse had been to fight and die rather than face the embarrassment of backing down and running. Without her and the children, she knew that John Robert's pride would have led him into a fight that he could never win. His heart and soul were invested in the home that he had built with his own hands and the family that he loved so much. Only the need to protect his family stopped him from certain death.

A flood of gratitude swept through Mary as the soldiers left them with the opportunity to escape. Her shoulder hurt and was drenched in blood from the wound, but she was proud that she had saved her husband. Now they would face the unknown together as they sought a new life. If they traveled farther into the Missouri countryside, they would be more protected from the terrible war.

John Robert bandaged Mary Owens's wound. The bullet had just grazed her shoulder, so it wasn't as serious as it looked. She would be all right. He knew that she had just saved his life. She meant more to him now than ever before.

Bravery

What is bravery? I don't know.
Is it fighting when you are scared?
Or is it just for show?
Not backing down when you are dared.

Maybe it's saving your family today,
Disregarding insults made to you,
Leave the fight and run away,
That is bravery too!

Leaving Home

They worked all day, packing everything useful that was left into the covered wagon parked at the back of the house. The little home on wheels was almost completely full now, except for the space for the children to ride and sleep behind the front seat. John Robert and Mary Owen hastily finished loading the wagon and hitched their four best horses to it. The last thing John Robert did before they left was to crawl under the house and retrieve his guns. He strapped his pistol in its holster onto his belt and laid his loaded shotgun and rifle next to his seat on the wagon. He would be prepared to defend his family if trouble came to them. He would be their protector as long as he was alive.

They didn't know where to go, but they headed the loaded covered wagon southeast toward the Ozark Mountains. They believed that the Federal Army would not go in that direction because the terrain was rough and the area was relatively unpopulated. The war had been moving into Missouri from northern Kansas, and battles were being fought on the western edge of Missouri. John Robert's family was now on the run, hoping to hide in the hills southeast of Cass County until it was safe to go back home.

Mary Owen fed the baby as she sat beside John Robert in the front seat of the covered wagon. The other two children, J. Belt and Pearlie, were back inside the wagon in their cozy spot lined with blankets and pillows, sleeping peacefully as the horses and wagon moved slowly down the road in the early morning light.

Mary Owen looked back once for a last view of the beautiful home that they had built together; she wanted to save the picture in her memory. Her face was grim, but she wouldn't let John Robert see her cry. She knew that he was near the breaking point, and her tears would only hurt him more. He was a good man. She would be strong for him, even though all they had now was hope and the few belongings that they had piled into the wagon.

For now, the Hammond family would try to live by supplementing their meager rations with the bounty of the Missouri countryside. Mary Owen had flour, cornmeal, canned vegetables and fruits, and miscellaneous supplies that the Federals had missed. The salt and sugar that she had saved would be good to have for flavoring their food. They had discovered one ham that had been hanging behind a curtain in the smokehouse and that the Federals had missed, so they knew that they could survive for a while on that. Five hens were tied up in the wagon and would produce eggs for them.

John Robert needed time to decide what to do and where to go. When the war was over, they would move back home and rebuild their lives—at least, that's what Mary Owen and John Robert believed at the time. The truth was that John Robert and Mary Owen were never again to live in their home in Cass County, Missouri.

Fear

It's losing all that we'd gained,
Our home and friends so true.
Without possessions, lives were strained.
Through mounting uncertainties, fear grew.

John Robert and Mary Owen had to go,
Finding as they left all behind,
Losing everything is only a show,
And fear is only in the mind.

The South Grand

The covered wagon lumbered slowly down the road, heading southeast and away from the threat of the Federal soldiers. It was a hot day, and John Robert's and Mary Owen's moods were somber as they thought about the abrupt change in their circumstances. Mary Owen was comforted by the fact that she was with John Robert; somehow, he always took care of her. He was very resourceful when it came to living off of the land. Her arm hurt where she had been wounded, but she knew that it would heal. A flesh wound was a small price to pay for saving John Robert.

Mary Owens's father was Dr. Hardin Rogers (pronounced "Ro-jair," as it was French). He lived in Bath County, Kentucky, and was a member of the Kentucky State Legislature. Dr. Rogers married Elizabeth Wilson in Kentucky on February 2, 1838. Their children were Mary Owen Rogers, born on November 3, 1840, and Agnes Rogers, who was born in May of 1843. Elizabeth, their mother, died in August of 1843.

Dr. Hardin Rogers then married Sarah Ann Thomas and united their families. They had three more children: Archer, Leslie, and Janie. Dr. Rogers died in 1852. At the time, the family was living in Cass County, Missouri.

Mary Owen Rogers married John Robert Hammond in Cass County on December 3, 1856. John Robert's brother Will, who was disabled and had bad legs, married Mary's sister Agnes. Will and John were both schoolteachers, and John taught school in Cass County.

Cass County was located thirty miles south of Kansas City, right over the Kansas state border in Missouri. The Hammond family settled in the country about ten miles south of Lone Jack. John and Mary often drove their wagon to the small town for supplies.

Now that the war was closing in on them, John and Mary were leaving their family home to save their lives. John had a plan for the near future. He was heading for a camping spot in the woods near the South Grand River that was hidden from the road. He had been fishing there before, and he thought that the horses could probably pull the wagon through the brush for about half a mile down to the river. He had an axe to clear the few trees that might be in their way, but the area was mostly covered in scrub brush and grass. The horses could graze there, and there would be plenty of water available.

The sun was setting as they pulled off of the road and headed toward the South Grand. John walked, leading the team of horses. The wagon followed the trail, bouncing over rocks. He slowed the wagon's wheels by pressing the brake boards against the wheel rims as they rolled down the hill toward the valley. The hidden area he sought had been forged by the river as it went through centuries of changes.

The South Grand ran down hills and sloped though the countryside. It grew as springs and creeks carved out valleys and joined it. The water fed the soil close by as it made its way toward larger rivers and then on toward the ocean. It was a good river. It ran clear and clean, and it contained good fish to eat and drew wildlife to it as they sought water to drink.

After the family made its way into the woods and was out of sight of the road, John Robert stopped the wagon and hitched the horses to a tree. Then he retraced their trail to the road. John Robert brushed over their tracks, hid the wheel marks, and straightened branches that had been bent and broken by the wagon when it had turned off the road and into the woods. He didn't want anyone to know that they were camped down by the river.

John Robert had learned his basic survival instincts from his forefathers. His hat was pulled tightly onto his head, and he wore his flannel shirt to protect him from the brush that they were traveling through. The mosquitoes would come out as the evening sun began to set. He would build a fire to ward them off. John Robert had been successful in the past because he had always adjusted and changed according to his circumstances in life. Now he had to call upon his every resource to overcome the new challenges that he and his family faced.

The family started moving forward again, and they soon spied the river. It was as John Robert remembered it. The water level was good, and there was an area of sand that made it easy to get to the water from the wagon. There were deeper pools both upstream and downstream of the shallow sand bar. They could wash and get water on the shallow riffle close by. The fishing would be good at night in the swift water that was running over the riffle; the fish swam into it to feed on minnows and crawfish. Tomorrow John Robert would dig some worms, seine minnows, and crawdads and prepare to set his lines out for the fish.

It was getting dark. John Robert leveled the covered wagon and braced the wheels with rocks from the edge of the river. He used more rocks to build a fire ring. The campfire he lit warmed them in the evening air. It also served as their stove, and Mary Owen heated up their supper.

John Robert tied short pieces of rope between the rear legs of the horses so that it would be difficult for them to walk. They could graze on grass and leaves and drink the water, but they wouldn't be able to wander off too far during the night. Hobbling the horses was a good way to keep them close by without tying them to a tree.

John Robert pulled some large logs close to the fire to sit on, and the family ate the ham and beans that Mary Owen had cooked. She brought out biscuits and jam for dessert. The meal was hot and good after a long day of travel and worry.

After a while of listening to the raccoons playing down by the river, the tired family climbed into their sleeping places in the wagon. John Robert, Mary Owen, and baby Hardin slept in the back of the wagon; John had unpacked some things and made a bed back there. J. Belt and Pearlie went to their space at the front of the wagon. The peaceful crackling of the fire and the sound of the flowing river lulled them to sleep.

The next morning, John Robert was already at the river fishing when the sun came up. Grabbing some cornbread and cheese, he walked down the trail to the river in the early light. He had some pieces of chicken liver saved in a jar; they would make good bait for catfish. The line on his fishing rod had a lead weight close to the hook, which kept the bait near the bottom of the river. The bottom, with its sunken rocks and brush to hide in, was where the big catfish fed.

John Robert found an old log to sit on and cast his bait into the pool below the swift current. He knew that the fish liked to wait in that area and eat the scraps of food that washed down the river. After a fifteen-minute wait, the line began to slowly move away from the end of the rod. The slack in the line began to tighten. He fed more line to the fish to make sure that it swallowed the bait. When the line was stretched tight, John Robert pulled the rod tip up hard to set the hook. The strong pull at the other end of his line told him that he had hooked a good fish.

The fish fought hard. John Robert let the line go out several times to wear the fish down and avoid breaking the line. Finally, the big cat tired. John Robert pulled it in, picked it up by its gill, and laid it on the riverbank.

"Not bad," John Robert thought to himself. He had caught a nice, six-pound channel cat that would make a good supper for the family. He baited the hook again and cast the bait in the same spot where he had caught the fish. His family wouldn't go hungry on that day!

Later that day, John Robert dug up some worms and set out five or six bank poles. He hoped to catch enough fish so that they could smoke them and have an ongoing supply of food. The bank poles stuck out of the riverbank, and the lines at the ends of the poles dipped baited hooks into the water. Fish would hook themselves during the night, and John could retrieve them the next morning.

That evening, John Robert went into the woods with his flintlock and shot three squirrels. They would be very tasty cooked in flour gravy after they had simmered over the fire for an hour or two.

Mary Owen fried the catfish in cornmeal, baked some potatoes beside the fire, and warmed up a pan of baked beans for their supper. Their food supply would hold out for a long time with the fish and game that John was bringing in.

Early the next morning, John saw some wood ducks swimming across the river. He loaded up his old flintlock shotgun, crept to the river, and hid behind some bushes. They were still there, swimming close together. Bang! Two ducks were down; he had shot a drake and a hen. The third wood duck, a hen, flew off; she would someday lay eggs to replace the ducks that John Robert had taken. He waded across the Grand on the shallow riffle to retrieve the ducks. The water was two feet deep and swift, but he reached the ducks and brought them back to the riverbank to clean them.

Looking at the beautiful drake with its blue, white, and green coloring and the hen with her soft, brown feathers, John Robert admired the beauty of the pair of ducks with a sense of sadness. They would fly no more, yet they would provide food for his family. He was thankful for the ducks and the food that they would provide. It was the endless dilemma of nature; John's love of birds and animals was mixed with the blessing of their bounty as food. John Robert understood that harvesting wild game was a necessary part in nature's evolutionary cycle.

Later that afternoon as John Robert watched the children, Mary Owen went into the woods and picked blackberries to make cobbler. She also found some walnuts and mulberries to supplement their diet.

One morning as John Robert was quietly fishing, he heard the sound of a large animal coming across the river toward him. The sounds of breaking sticks and the jingle of a saddle and harness were getting closer as he sat still with his back resting against a tree.

Through the woods on the other side of the river, John saw a blue coat and recognized that it belonged to a Federal soldier who was riding toward the river across from him. "The soldier must be a scout searching the area for Confederate sympathizers; he must have decided to water his horse," he thought to himself.

John slowly reached behind his back and took his loaded flintlock rifle from where it was leaning against the tree. He lifted the rifle to his shoulder and aimed at the blue coat. The Federal saw his movement and quickly jumped down from his horse. A moment later, a shot from the man's rifle splintered the tree close to John's left ear. John could see the man frantically working to reload his flintlock rifle. He knew that he had ten to twenty seconds to fire back across the river before the Federal would be ready to fire at him again.

Sighting in on the patch of blue that he could see through the bushes, John gave his barrel a slight elevation to compensate for the drop of the bullet and gently squeezed the trigger. The crack of the shot combined with the kick of the gun sent the lead bullet across the South Grand toward that blue patch of cloth that was showing through the bushes. The sound of a thud and something crumpling in the brush told John that his bullet had hit its mark. Now the air was still and quiet. He could only hear the gentle gurgling of the river in the shot's aftermath.

John reloaded his gun, and after waiting fifteen minutes, he carefully waded across the river to where the man in the blue coat lay. The red spot on his chest told John that his shot had dealt the man a fatal blow. He felt sick inside. He'd had no choice in the matter, but he hated the war now more than ever. The killing was so senseless.

Leaving the soldier on the ground where he had fallen, John hurried across the river and walked swiftly back to camp. "Mary, we have to pack up fast and leave this place. I just shot a Federal soldier. It was either him or me," he said.

Mary sensed John's urgency. They packed up the wagon quickly, put the children in their spot inside, and went through the brush up to the road. Turning the wagon southwest, the family headed deeper into the Missouri hills, hoping that they wouldn't be followed. They needed to find a safe area to live in and a means of survival. Because Mary Owen was pregnant, they would also need a warm house to stay in during the winter.

After about ten days of travel, John Robert and Mary Owen arrived at a little town on the Osage River. It was Osceola, Missouri.

As luck would have it, there was a teaching position open at a grade school in the country a few miles out of town. After an interview, John Robert was hired, and the family rented a small house not far from the school. People in the area seemed friendly, and they would be safer from the war here. The Hammond family had arrived in St. Clair County, Missouri. Over time, John Robert and Mary

Owen—my great grandparents through their son Hardin—would firmly establish my ancestors in that area.

The River

Life's blood flows through field and farm,
Ever nourishing all life around.
Nature's beauty glows with special charm,
While plants, animals, and fish abound.

Keep flowing with your beauty rare,
You mean so much to me.
The moonlit waters shine brightly there
As you wander past to reach the sea.

A New Home

St. Clair County is an area in southwestern Missouri that has a haunting wilderness and also a wonderful history. The hills are low and stretch out into fields and valleys that have been cut out of the scrub oaks, hickory trees, and tangled brush. Early settlers created pastureland and later farmland so that they could make a living.

If one knew the plants and trees in that area, bountiful forest foods were available to help sustain both animal and human life. Sprinkled throughout the forests were pawpaw, persimmon, and mulberry trees that bore fruit.

The pawpaw, when ripe, is a banana-shaped fruit that starts out green but turns yellow in the fall as it ripens. It doesn't taste much like a banana and has a large seed that takes up most of the fruit on the inside, but the outer shell and flesh of the fruit are edible. For a hungry traveler in the fall woods, pawpaws were ripe for picking and eating.

The persimmon trees yield small, red fruits that are full of seeds. The little, round fruits hang on the trees throughout the fall season until some animal, such as a raccoon or possum, eats them. The persimmon fruits are sweet and good when ripe.

Of course, blackberries, raspberries, serviceberries, and elderberries were also available throughout the woods. Many a cobbler and pie were made from the blackberries and raspberries. Elderberry wine is sweet-tasting and easy to make in the fall. Residents in the area loved to brew the wine for their own enjoyment.

Walnut and hickory trees also yielded food in the forest, and the hazelnut bushes in the area produced good nuts. Collecting the nuts in the fall and storing them in a dry place yielded tasty treats during the winter. People could also eat acorns from the many oak trees, but only if they boiled them for many hours to remove the bitter taste of tannin. Acorns were the last things a person would want to eat from the nut family in Missouri. Still, if you were starving, they were available as food in the fall and winter.

The soil in western Missouri is sandy and rocky. Some valleys contain a layer of topsoil consisting of black dirt, but the area was formed millions of years ago when the Ozark Mountains rose up from the inner earth and brought the rocks and sandy soil with them. This special area of land in western Missouri is best described as the foothills of the Ozark Mountains.

In the early 1800's, Americans found their way to this wild and undeveloped part of the world. In some cases, they migrated from Kentucky, finding cheap land and bountiful streams and forests. One could live just by harvesting the fish and wildlife that were so abundant in the region at that time. Deer and turkeys were excellent game, and the hunter who brought game home was always highly regarded by his family. Smoked deer especially would often last a family through the winter.

In addition to keeping chickens and cows, families could eke out a living from the poor ground by growing large gardens. The gardens needed periodic watering, so growing healthy vegetables was hard work, but having the gardens helped people add a lot of healthful food to their diets throughout the year. People also grew and stacked hay to provide food for their livestock during the winter months. Even with its rocks and sandy soil, western Missouri offered a new life to the adventurous and hardy.

Somehow, John Robert and Mary Owen carved out their existence in this rough area of the world. They lived through droughts and cold winters, cleared land, lost children to illnesses, and generally survived and lived good lives throughout the early history of our country. Thanks to John Robert and Mary Owen, many of my ancestors were born, lived, and died within a fifty-mile radius of the little river town called Osceola. The town was named after the Osceola Indians who had populated that land so long ago. Osceola was located on the Osage River. It had a town square featuring a county courthouse in its center. The small town was the closest thing to the civilized world that my grandparents—and in their early years, my mother and father—knew.

About seven miles northwest of Osceola was another small town called Lowry City. It was smaller than Osceola and had a single main street, but it was located on the plains and was a good place to market crops back then. Lowry City during the 1860s was a friendly little town where neighbors relied upon each other for assistance.

Closer to the homes of my grandparents was a small settlement named Chalk Level, which had a general store. Chalk Level was about seven miles from both Osceola and Lowry City; it depended on which road you traveled.

My father and his parents lived one mile down a gravel road from Chalk Level. My mother and her parents lived about three and a half miles from Chalk Level. Their lives eventually came together, and they ended up as husband and wife.

St. Clair County, Missouri

People took what land that they could acquire and made the best of their lives in that harsh part of the world. I owe my soul to their acceptance of their world as it was then and their stalwart perseverance in the face of the obstacles they encountered during those very difficult and trying times.

The story of my mother's father, Hardin Rogers Hammond, and the life he lived gives insight into my heritage and the values that have been passed down through the generations of our family.

Destiny

Chance plus desire take us there
As we seek our future strong.
Families come with love and care
To forget the war so wrong.

We find happiness in our new place,
Using skills learned long ago.
Starting is tough, but keeping the pace,
Our new home begins to grow.

After the War

After several years, the Civil War soldiers finally moved out of Cass County. John Robert and Mary Owen rode back in their covered wagon to see their former home. They were shocked to find that the Federal soldiers had burned their beautiful Cass County home to the ground. The ugly pile of ashes and the old fireplace and chimney that were still standing were all that remained of their previous home. The loss brought tears to Mary's eyes and a lump to John's throat. Yet they had been among the lucky ones. So many of their former neighbors and friends from the area were now dead or wandering penniless, never understanding why the war had to happen in the first place. Cass County and the families that lived there had been changed forever by the war.

Digging up little Willie's casket was heart-wrenching for John Robert, but they had decided that it belonged with them, where they could pay their respects at his graveside. Mary Owen wanted his remains closer to her in Osceola. Her love for little Willie had remained constant within her heart throughout the four years that they had been gone.

On the way back, Mary opened the casket for one last look. Only four brass buttons from the little coat he had been buried in remained. They were nestled in the dust covering the bottom of the casket. Willie's physical presence had left this earth. Mary was only consoled by her belief that Willie's soul was now in heaven.

The Hammonds returned to St. Clair County and bought a house and a farm called Woodland Home. They settled on that farm, which was four miles northwest of Osceola. John Robert periodically taught school at the Chalk Level School and the Pleasant Valley School in St. Clair County. The family stayed in this area but found it challenging to rebuild their lives in a new environment after the Civil War. Many times their progress in life was disappointing, but there had been no other choice for them.

The Past

The people and things we hope to find
Are locked in memories' embrace.
The reality of change works on our mind,
What was never is, going back to that place.

Deep inside we want the same;
Its familiar comforts soothe our soul.
Burned house, cold casket, a sad, sad, game.
In finding the truth, the trip took its toll.

Young Hardin

Hardin loved to roam the fields and woods that surrounded Woodland Home when he was growing up. He explored the creeks and valleys with J. Belt, his older brother, and brought home turtles, crawdads, small fish, and even a chipmunk that they caught in a trap.

John Robert had made a box trap for the boys. The bait, usually chicken entrails, would be placed at the far end of the rectangular box. A notched stick went through a hole in the top of the wooden box in the back, right in front of the bait. There was a door that slid up and down on a track inside the open end. When they lifted the door up, the notch in the stick would catch on a hole in the top of the box. When the animal entered the box to get the bait, it would hit the stick holding up the door and release it. The animal would then be caught until the boys checked the trap.

Since it was a live trap without any holes or windows, they never knew what they had caught until they opened the trap door. This moment was always exciting. Anything, including raccoons or snakes, could set the trap off. Sometimes the animal got away, but one time they caught a possum and brought it home to show John Robert. Then they turned it loose.

Pearlie liked to fish. She often walked with the boys down to the creek carrying a can of worms. They all spent summer afternoons together. The small perch and chub minnows pulled their fishing corks under the water, and they yanked the poles up to set the hooks. The small ones were hard to hook, but it was exciting when they hooked one of the yellow bullheads that roamed the bottom in the deeper water. That was something that they could take home to eat.

Sometimes a large crawdad would be hanging onto the bait when they pulled their lines out of the water. The skinned tails of the crawdads made good bait for the larger bullheads.

When Hardin once hooked a snake, Pearlie was scared. The snake's white cotton mouth would be deadly if it bit them. J. Belt cut the line with his pocket-knife, and the snake disappeared, wiggling down through the murky brown water of Cooper's Creek.

Hardin developed and grew in the wilderness of western Missouri. The environment, with its combination of hardship and beauty, became part of his identity. The natural rhythm of the land that provided his family with pleasure and food became ingrained within him.

Youth

The best time in life is growing,
When life's newness fills our minds.
Free as the river waters flowing,
Cares are lessened and life is kind.

It's time to breathe in fresh air,
Experience our minds and bodies change.
Find friends and love, take a dare.
Through life's possibilities we will range.

Finding the Road

There were also hard times for the family, and they made Hardin very sad. Of Mary Owen's and John Robert Hammond's thirteen children, only five reached adulthood. The children who had survived so far were Pearlie, Ada, Claude, J. Belt, and Hardin. But one more death came only too soon and too tragically.

Pearlie, with her long, brown hair and blue eyes, died at the age of eighteen and was the hardest to lose. Pearlie was a very good whistler, and she was Hardin's favorite. Her last words were, "Lay me down on my left side." Her father complied, and beautiful Pearlie gently passed away. She most likely died of tuberculosis.

In 1875, when Pearlie died, Hardin was just fourteen years old. He had loved his beautiful sister and friend. She had been so much fun to be with. They had ridden their horses out to Cooper's Creek to fish and talk so many times. Hardin could talk to Pearlie about girls he knew and about how bad he felt about the brothers and sisters that he had lost. She had been his anchor in life.

Hardin kept a calendar picture in his room of a very pretty young woman who reminded him of Pearlie. Later, the family's cows broke into the cemetery and destroyed some of the tombstones, including hers. John Robert and Mary Owen kept a piece of Pearlie's tombstone in an upstairs room in her remembrance.

The day of Pearlie's funeral, the tightness in his chest made Hardin feel like crying his heart out. He knew that Missouri men were supposed to be tough, but down deep inside his heart, Hardin knew that Pearlie was gone. All that he had left were the memories of her bright and loving presence. She had watched over him as he was growing up. He would never forget Pearlie and her kindness to him.

After laying her to rest in the Concord Cemetery next to the church, the family and Pearlie's friends all gathered at the Hammond's Woodland Home to discuss Pearlie's life and grieve. It was a bad time for Hardin's father and mother.

They had now lost nine children since they had married in 1856. Losing Pearlie was another crushing blow to the whole family.

After an hour or so with the family, Hardin knew that he wanted to be alone to think about his memories and try to understand just how to accept his sister's death. He saddled up his brown and white pony, Brownie, and rode down the trail and across the bridge over Cooper's Creek where he and Pearlie had had so much fun fishing and laughing.

Hardin and Brownie headed up the sloping hill to the picnic spot on Bald Knob that he and Pearlie had loved so much. He went through the open pasture, past the large and gentle cattle resting and eating the tall grass, and wound through the scrub oaks until he reached the top of the highest hill in the area. Brownie stopped, and Hardin sat in the saddle quietly, trying to make sense of his life. The clouds hung low and seemed oppressive on that dark day, and time seemed to stand still.

As he thought about Pearlie, Hardin found comfort is his memories of her. She had laughed at him when he had done stupid things. He had talked with her about his frustrations with his life, and she had shown a special caring and compassion that had comforted him.

Hardin would never truly get over losing Pearlie. The memories of her would never leave him. He knew that her spirit would be with him always; she could never be taken away from his heart. If Hardin went to heaven, she would be there. Hardin knew that he must live a good life, the best one possible, so that when the time came, he would be reunited with Pearlie up there. It was the hope that he had been searching for. Yes, he would do his best during his lifetime and make her proud of his accomplishments.

Hardin would always love Pearlie. Her vital spirit would remain with him forever.

Pearlie

Pearlie Hammond died so tragically.
Gone were her spirit and love so kind.
Hardin felt the loss and couldn't see
How to justify her death in his mind.

Buried now beneath cold ground,
Her spirit left earth for skies of blue.

Hardin's only thought was to close out the sound,
Seek silence to remember love so true.

Growing Up

Hardin and Frank sat in the soft glow of the candlelight in the bat room at Monegaw Cave. Frank had some whisky that he had taken from the barn on his parents' farm. Hardin was fourteen, and Frank was a year older. They had thought that they would try some alcohol to see why the adults made such a fuss about it. Frank was a big boy at six foot one, and he had a way with the girls. They liked his recklessness and his handsome features. Frank was, as usual, describing his exploits and conquests as Hardin listened intently.

Hardin worshipped his friend and looked up to him. Frank was well liked by their friends, but many parents disapproved of Frank's somewhat lazy lifestyle. His bragging was infused with exaggeration and sometimes contained downright lies. Hardin didn't have a way with the ladies, and so he liked to hear Frank tell stories that were interesting and romantic at the same time. They'd just had a few sips of the whisky. Hardin thought it had tasted awful, but he could still feel its slightly numbing effects as they mounted their horses for the ride home.

It was dark as they rode over the dirt road that cut through to the main road leading to Hardin's parents' home, Woodland Hills. Frank lived with his father on a small farm a few miles past Woodland Hills. Frank's mother had passed away two years ago. He and his father lived a pretty rough life without a woman to take care of them.

Flashes of lightning and thunder foretold of the thunderstorm that was fast overtaking them. It hit with strong winds and heavy rain. Missouri thunderstorms could be vicious, so they sought shelter from the storm in the old, deserted schoolhouse at the intersection of the roads. They were already soaked by the time they jumped off of their horses and ran up under the porch roof that held back the driving rain.

Just as the drenched young men were starting to sit down on the porch and settle in to wait out the storm, a terrible moaning noise came from within the schoolhouse. What could it be? They heard it again, even over the sound of the driving rain on the old schoolhouse roof. It was an "Aooooooahhhaaaaa" sound that sent shivers down their spines. Then a flowing, white apparition appeared in the doorway behind them and floated toward them. It was coming to get them!

They didn't have to the think twice; the rainstorm was inviting compared to the ghost coming after them. Hardin vowed never to drink whisky again as they jumped on their horses and raced for home. Something was in that schoolhouse. The apparition had come floating through the door. It had come right at them. They didn't know what it was, but they weren't staying around to find out.

The next morning, Hardin told his dad, John Robert, about the ghost in the schoolhouse. They decided to ride back and see just what or who could be in there. It wasn't as scary in broad daylight. John Robert gently pushed the door open and looked inside.

There in the corner of the old room was a gray-haired woman, probably in her seventies, sound asleep on the floor. She had a white robe on with "Osceola Nursing Home" embroidered upon the front lapel. "This must be the woman who escaped from the nursing home," John Robert said. "She needs to go back there."

The Young Missourians

They woke her up. She didn't know where she was, but she was thankful that someone had found her. John Robert waited at the schoolhouse and watched her while Hardin rode home and got the buggy. Then they rode into Osceola and turned the woman over to the manager of the nursing home.

Hardin began to realize that there was an explanation for everything one encountered in life. Even what appeared to be a ghost was really only an old woman who had escaped from the nursing home. He had learned that things are not always what they appeared to be. One needed to investigate and get the facts to find out the real truths in life. It was a good, practical lesson.

Friendship

Young men seeking to explore,
To learn and experience every day,
They find surprises wait in store
For reality to explain away.

Excitement, thrills, and mysteries
Challenge the senses and the mind.
Growing together, building histories,
Finding true friendships of a higher kind.

Birthday Present

Hardin's fifteenth birthday was April 7, 1876. His mother, Mary Owen, told Hardin that they wanted to have a little birthday celebration for him at dinnertime. She and John Robert had also been discussing his future and wanted to talk to him about it. Hardin wondered what they were thinking about, but he knew that they both wanted to be there to present their ideas to him. He would be graduating from high school in a few weeks, and Hardin hadn't really made any plans or even thought about his future.

Hardin was content just working for a local farmer who was raising cattle and hogs for the market. What little money he made helped the family out and provided Hardin with spending money. He had learned a great deal about how to run a stock farm over the past two years, and he loved to be outside in nature as much as possible. In his spare time, Hardin hunted in the winter and fished in the summer. He used his father's old double-barreled flintlock shotgun or the flintlock rifle that had been in the family for a long time. The family almost always had meat for dinner, often because of the game Hardin brought home.

The Missouri countryside was mostly safe, but reports of roadside robberies and occasional killings were becoming more and more commonplace. People had to be careful when they met strangers on the road. Most everyone carried guns when they traveled—even if they didn't need them for protection, they needed guns to shoot game. Deer were plentiful out in the country. Hardin was always careful, but he was growing into a man. He would now be treated as an adult by any stranger he encountered on the road.

That evening, Mary Owen prepared a special dinner of all Hardin's favorites: mashed potatoes, green beans, breaded pork chops with gravy, and a nice white cake with chocolate frosting. His siblings, Ada, J. Belt, and Claude, had made sure to be there for Hardin's birthday. They loved him and even had small gifts. J. Belt gave him a belt buckle. Ada had knitted him a nice warm, red scarf, and Claude had used his special talent of whittling to make Hardin a wooden flute to play. It was a wonderful birthday dinner with a lot of laughs and entertaining stories. The party was a great success.

Just when Hardin thought the party was almost over, John Robert went into the back bedroom and came out with a long, slim package wrapped in brown paper. "Happy birthday, Hardin," John Robert said.

Hardin took the package, which was heavy. He couldn't imagine what it was. Tearing the wrapper off, Hardin discovered that it was something he had always wanted but never thought he would own. It was a classic 1860 Henry rifle. This was the kind of repeating rifle that the troops had used near the end of the Civil War. It was well oiled, had a lever-action shell ejection system, and shot a .44-caliber bullet.

The Henry rifle was prized because the lever ejection system allowed it to shoot sixteen shots in rapid succession without being reloaded. It would be a great hunting rifle and was good for protecting himself too. It was also compact, so Hardin could ride with it in his saddle scabbard wherever he went. Hardin felt tears well up in his eyes as he examined the rifle. He knew that John Robert must have saved for quite a while to buy it for him.

"Thank you all for such a fine birthday. I hope to make you proud of me," Hardin said with sincere emotion.

"I'm glad that you like the rifle," John Robert said. "Your mother and I think that you should have it because we are sending you to Quincy to go to business school next fall. You have always been a good student. With another year of education, you can teach school or go into some type of business. The Quincy business school has a good reputation. They have arranged boarding in a private home for you. Your mother and I want you to have a good education so that you can build a sound foundation for your future."

Hardin was excited that he would be going away to school, but he knew that he would miss his family and friends. It was a big step for the fifteen-year-old, but he was confident that he was strong and smart enough to live in Quincy while he got his education. He had until August to prepare himself for the trip and for any challenges that might arise during the coming year.

Hardin had planned to work for Ory Sutter, who owned the store in Chalk Level. He could still tend Ory's stock for him during the summer and save his money for school. He would also practice as much as possible with the Henry rifle. Then if he met highwaymen on the road, he would have a chance of outshooting them.

Hardin took nothing for granted. He would prepare himself as well as possible for the unknown obstacles that he may meet. His future was becoming clearer, and he would do his best to become successful and make his family proud. In the coming year, Hardin would be glad that he had prepared himself so thoroughly; that year would prove to be more challenging and dangerous than he had ever imagined it would.

Hardin would soon turn from a boy into a man overnight, proving himself in many ways where others would have failed. Somehow, he would find the physical and mental strength to overcome the obstacles and dangers in his path.

Life's Truth

He changed and grew, his youth was gone,
Strong, healthy, and with a quick mind.
Hardin's family pushed him on,
Seeking life's truth was his to find.

More knowledge he would always seek.
Dangerous adventures followed too.
Deep inside, his soul would peak,
Finding love and success that rang true.

Time To Go

It was August, and the time came for Hardin and Brownie to make the long trip across Missouri to Quincy, Illinois. Hardin was planning to study for a business degree. The last family dinner was a quiet one; each brother, sister, and parent silently wondered about the dangerous trip that Hardin would make. They knew that life would be different at home without his cheerful presence around the farm. They were worried about his safety, but they knew that he was capable and smart. He was the best shot with his rifle in those parts and could even match a pistol draw out of the scabbard on his saddle. Yes, Hardin could take care of himself if anyone could.

After supper, John Robert asked Hardin to ride up to Old Baldy with him. John Robert wanted to spend a last few precious moments with his son before Hardin set out on his perilous journey. It was time to transfer the Hammond family philosophy and wisdom to Hardin. John Robert wanted to give his son the knowledge he would need to form the basis for a good and rewarding life.

The sun was starting to drop lower in the sky as Hardin and his father sat down on a log facing Pleasant Valley. Far off down the hill, Cooper's Creek was a trail of water running through the fields, and the gentle presence of the cattle gave the summer evening an atmosphere of peacefulness. The two men sat silent for quite a while, soaking in the beauty of the evening and the worshipful atmosphere that God had made. There was a silent bond between father and son that would last forever.

"I want you to know that I love you very much," John Robert finally said. "No matter how far away you are or how your life is going, I will always love you. If you are sick or in trouble, you must write to me so that I can come and help. Always remember, Hardin—you are a precious son, and you have many friends and relatives who want you to be healthy and happy throughout your lifetime."

John Robert paused here and carefully looked over the young man who sat where his little boy had been not too long ago. Hardin's direct gaze and muscular features were evidence of the inner strength that he had developed during the past year.

John Robert walked over to his horse and pulled a brown envelope out of the saddlebag. "Hardin, here is something that I want you to keep always. Sometimes it is easier to write thoughts down, especially when you have something important to say."

The envelope had his name—Hardin R. Hammond—on the front. Hardin pulled the letter out of the envelope; the flawless penmanship gave the letter a professional and artful appearance. Hardin could see that it was carefully written. As John Robert anxiously watched him, Hardin began to read.

> Dear Hardin,
>
> Always be true to yourself and your inner feelings. Only you can know deep inside what is right and what is wrong. Always act upon your own instincts. You must always be honest with yourself. People will respect you for it and look to you for advice. Honesty and truthfulness are the basis for a person's happiness in life. You may be tempted to conceal little facts that you should be sharing or to be dishonest. Don't ever become a person who does that! Openness and helpfulness will always be rewarded.
>
> Each day that we are alive, we can make a difference within ourselves and to others around us. Treasure your friendships, and be someone who people can always count on to follow through with your promises. Do your best to do a good job at whatever task is at hand. Follow your heart and not just your friends' ideas of how you should live your life.
>
> Reach out to other people. Many are shy or do not know how to express their true feelings. Draw them out, and try to reach a deeper understanding of each person you meet. Be interested in them, not just in yourself. You will find that each person has good reason to be how he or she is. Go behind each person's facade and find their true feelings. Only then will you find true friends and understand them in ways that will mean so much to you throughout your lifetime.
>
> There are bad people in this country. If someone threatens you or harms you, take swift and decisive action against him. You have Brownie, as smart a horse as any I know of, and you have the Henry rifle. I'm proud that you have become such a crack shot with that rifle. If you have to use it on another man to protect yourself or someone that you love, do not hesitate,

but let your shots ring true. Be sure that you know the bad from the good, and always protect yourself from the bad elements of this country.

You will fall in love someday. You'll know it when the time comes. Be respectful to your wife and children, and love them while understanding any faults they may have. A man's family brings him satisfaction that he can find nowhere else. Always set a good example and hold high standards. Your family will follow in whatever footprints you choose to leave.

When you are far away and lonely, take this letter out and read it to yourself. In this way, I will always be near you, no matter where you are.

Love always,
John Robert

The evening was entering its twilight phase. Soon they would have to ride down the hill together for what would be the last time for a long while. Hardin carefully replaced the letter in its envelope and held it tightly in his hand. The words his father had written had touched him deeply.

"Yes, father; thank you for your wisdom and advice. I promise you that I will do my very best in school and also in my life. I would like to adopt a motto for my life that will always remind me of the path that I have chosen. It is 'Endeavor to do right!' I will always live my life according to this ideal and keep with me your thoughtful and important advice."

Hardin turned and hugged John Robert with his heart full of love. He would always treasure this powerful moment in his life. The knowledge of how much John Robert loved him gave him the strength to meet the challenges that would come in his future.

Hardin and John Robert mounted their horses and rode slowly down the hill called Old Baldy, through the fields, and across the bridge over Cooper's Creek as the light finally gave way to darkness. Tomorrow Hardin's adventure would begin. He was excited and prepared for the long journey that awaited him. It was time to go!

Guidance

It was a special time for father and son,
Knowledge and advice passed there.

John Robert gave Hardin his words and a gun,
Truth, honesty, and safety showed concerned care.

A son needs to listen and set his sights
On what he expects to do.
For time passes swiftly from days to nights,
Then your son leaves home and you.

Traveling to Quincy

Hardin was packed early the next morning. Mary Owen had made up a cloth sack of food and utensils for him to take on his journey. Quincy, Illinois, was 180 miles away. It would take Hardin one week to ride Brownie over the hilly dirt roads and through small towns to get there. John Robert had sent Hardin's trunk with his clothes and violin on the train to be delivered to Quincy. He had also arranged for a room for Hardin that was close to the school.

Hardin had saved some money to take on the trip. He also had his knife, one hundred bullets for his Henry rifle, and fishing line and hooks to catch fish to eat when he could. He also had a bedroll tied behind his saddle and extra clothes and rain gear tied behind that. Brownie was looking more and more like a pack horse and less and less like the saddle horse he really was.

The family came out of the house to watch Hardin ride off. As he started to ride around the corner, they all waved good-bye and wished him luck. Brownie's shod hooves clattered on the boards of the bridge over Cooper's Creek, and they stayed on the road going east instead of turning to climb the path up to Bald Knob. The air was filled with the quiet thud of hooves on the dirt road. Hardin was surrounded by the special kind of silence that can only be felt as one rides alone through the Missouri hills and woods.

Hardin knew for the first time what real loneliness was. Leaving his parents and brothers and sister behind was the hardest thing he had ever done. He would miss their support, advice, and love more than anything else.

Hardin and Brownie followed the road away from home and toward the unknown life that was waiting for them. The long trip promised unexpected challenges, but Hardin was a Missouri boy and was self-sufficient and strong. He had a good horse and a gun, and he certainly wouldn't go hungry with his fishing and hunting skills to supplement the food that Mary Owen had packed.

He would get his education in Quincy. Educated men in western Missouri were few and far between. His best friend, Frank Hall, was cleaning at Teal's Bar and helping local farmers in order to earn a living. But Hardin would be home in a year with an education, and he would use it to earn money and eventually buy a stock farm. He knew that he was on the right path. His father and mother had given him an opportunity, and now he would make the best of it.

The August sun grew hotter as Brownie walked briskly down the road. Around noon, Hardin began to get hungry. When he came to a creek running along the road, he stopped and let Brownie graze and drink water while he ate the sandwich that Mary Owen had packed. He also had an apple to eat for dessert. After about thirty minutes, Hardin mounted up and headed out again down the dusty road.

Hardin wore a Missouri straw hat to keep away the effects of the hot sun. He also had on a light, long-sleeved shirt so that his arms wouldn't get too sunburned from the hot and sultry day. Brownie was sweating, but the little horse kept up a steady pace, and the scrub oaks and hickory trees slowly rolled by. Once in a while Hardin saw a squirrel or a few birds, but it was proving to be a long, hard ride in the steamy, hot weather.

Later that afternoon, he passed a small boy with no shirt or shoes. Looking down, Hardin could see that the boy had been crying. "Where are you going?" Hardin asked.

Traveling from Osceola to Quincy

"I'm sick, and I'm going home," the boy answered. "I was fishing in the stream over yonder, but I'm not feeling good, so I'm heading home."

Hardin could see that the boy was shaky and pale. He didn't look well. "How far is it?" Hardin asked.

"My home is about three miles down the road. I think that I can make it," the boy said.

Hardin handed the boy his canteen and gave him a drink of water. The boy gulped it down. Hardin could tell that he was having a hard time.

"What is your name? Hardin asked.

"Billy," the boy answered.

"Well, good luck, Billy. I hope you feel better," Hardin said as he rode on down the road.

As Hardin rode away from the boy, he started thinking about what his father had said many times: always do what you know in your heart is right. Put yourself in the other person's place. Seek to understand others by thinking about how their lives are and by being interested in them and what they have to say. It was the golden rule that he had learned in church: do unto others as you would have them do unto you. Endeavor to do right. The boy needed help. He was little and sick. Hardin knew what he had to do.

The boy was surprised to see the brown and white horse and its rider coming back toward him. Hardin turned Brownie around and said, "Billy, get up behind me in the saddle. I'll take you home."

The boy climbed up on Brownie and held onto Hardin. Hardin could feel the tears wet against his shirt as the boy cried with gratefulness. When Hardin dropped him off in front of a small, run-down shack house three miles down the road, Billy looked up at Hardin and said, "Thank you, mister. I think that I'll be alright now." Then the boy walked up the path and went into the house.

Hardin felt good. He had lost a little time, but he had helped someone who had needed it. "Endeavor to do right" would always be the motto by which he lived.

That evening, Hardin made a little fire, cooked some supper, and rolled up in his bedroll for a good night's sleep. Before he went to sleep, he took John Robert's letter out of the saddlebag he was using as a pillow and read it again by the firelight. John Robert's loving letter gave Hardin a peaceful feeling as he lay alone in his bedroll in the wilderness. Familial love transcends all distances. With the Henry rifle close under his bedroll, he was comforted by John Robert's thoughtful words.

It had been a long day but a good day. Sleep came fast.

Values

An important part of living well
Is helping others in need.
Sometimes our hard decisions tell
How we chose to do a good deed.

One of the greatest rewards in life
Is gratitude, they say.
Lend a hand, ease someone's strife,
Feel good about yourself today.

Trouble on the Road

Hardin woke up at the first light of day to the morning twittering and chirping of the woodland birds. Brownie was grazing on some grass close by and came over to be saddled when Hardin called him.

"Eat three good meals every day," John Robert had said. "A man's body needs fuel to do hard work and to stay healthy."

Hardin peeled two boiled eggs and ate them with a couple slices of cooked bacon and a big square of cornbread for breakfast. Then he went down to the creek, took off his shirt, and washed up with soap and water. By 6:30 AM, he had mounted up on Brownie and was headed on down the road in the early morning mist. The morning went by fast. Hardin ate some beef jerky and an apple as he rode along around noontime.

In the early afternoon, Hardin saw two riders coming toward him from the opposite direction. As they came closer, Hardin saw that they wore pistols and looked pretty rough. Both had beards and wore cowboy hats, and they looked as if they meant to talk to him.

The men pulled up when they came close to Hardin and Brownie. Hardin put one hand down on the Henry rifle and levered a bullet into the firing position. If there was going to be trouble, he wanted to be ready.

"Nice little paint you're riding," the taller of the two men said.

"Where are you headed, son?" the smaller of the two asked as he spit chewing tobacco down at Brownie's feet.

"I'm headed to Quincy to go to school and study business," Hardin answered. He didn't like the looks of these men at all. They were hard and most likely looking to steal his horse and money. These were the type of men John Robert had warned Hardin about.

"If you do have to protect yourself, act fast, and shoot like you mean it," John Robert had advised.

The men didn't miss his hand on the rifle.

"They are the types that find it easier to sneak up on somebody, or worse, shoot them in the back," thought Hardin.

"Well, I think that I will ride on down the road. I've got a hard ride ahead of me. I'll see you fellows later," Hardin said.

The smaller man spit more tobacco down by Brownie's feet. Brownie looked down at the small wad of tobacco and spit in the dirt, then raised his head again. Hardin could feel the alertness in the little horse. He sensed danger.

"Yeah, better get going. It's a long way to Quincy. It can be dangerous too." The man had a smirk on his face when he said it.

Hardin felt fear deep inside. If they tried to rob him now, he had a chance with his rifle. But if they followed him, they would most likely come after him in the dark.

Hardin turned and started walking Brownie down the road. The men sat on their horses without even pretending to continue in the direction they had been traveling. They were still there talking to each other when Hardin and Brownie rounded the bend in the road.

"They will probably follow me," Hardin thought.

He glanced back now and then and saw dust in the distance from their horses. He would have to be ready after dark. He was sure that they planned to rob him; they probably meant to kill him too. Out there in the country, no one would ever catch them. He was in a tight spot.

That night, Hardin stopped by another creek as soon as it got dark. He built a fire and cooked some supper. Still he saw no sign of the men.

After supper, he put his bedroll near the fire and stuffed it with grass and sticks. He put the saddle where his head usually went and put some more wood on the fire. He wanted it to burn brightly late into the night. Then he climbed up the hill and sat with his back to a big tree. He had built the fire on the other side of the bedroll so that if they approached it, thinking that he was in it, he would be able to see to shoot. Brownie was tied up off to the side. If they tried to steal him, they would have a hard time getting the rope loose. Brownie was close enough to the light to allow Hardin to see him. It looked like it was going to be a long night.

Around midnight, Hardin heard a faint rustle and saw some movement down by the campsite. It looked like one man was trying to untie Brownie while the other sneaked up on the bedroll. The man had his gun in his hand and was pointing it at the bedroll. Hardin aimed the Henry at the man who was untying Brownie.

Everything happened at once. While the man at the bedroll shot into it, Hardin shot the man untying Brownie in the leg. He screamed and went down.

Then Hardin turned his rifle on the man at the bedroll and shot him in the shoulder. As the man shouted and grabbed his shoulder, Hardin put another shot in his leg, and he fell by the fire.

"Throw your guns out now!" Hardin yelled.

The man by Brownie hesitated, and Hardin laid a shot into the dirt inches from his head. That convinced both of the robbers to get rid of their guns.

Hardin came down out of the woods. The men didn't have any fight left in them. He tied them up to a tree with his rope. Then he saddled Brownie, picked up his bedroll and pans, and headed on down the road.

At daybreak, Hardin came to the next town, which was Sedalia. When he found the sheriff, Hardin told him about the men and where they were. "From your description, I know those men," the sheriff said. "We have been trying to catch them for bank robbery and murder. You were lucky to outsmart them!"

"If you don't mind, Sheriff, I'm pretty tired. Maybe I can get a room and get some sleep. I'll be glad to identify them and sign a sworn statement before I go on my way to Quincy."

"That's okay with me, Hardin. I'll get a couple of deputies and ride out for them this morning. After they are doctored up and in jail, we will get your statement, and you can be on your way."

With Brownie at the livery stable and Hardin in a soft bed in the rooming house, he was finally safe and began to fall to sleep. He thought about the robbers and how he had outsmarted them. Of course, he'd had luck on his side or things might have turned out otherwise.

John Robert would have been proud of the way Hardin had handled himself. You never knew what to expect on those Missouri country roads.

Danger

When faced with danger, we must decide.
Think fast, and know what to do.
Save your life and turn the tide.
Now it's either me or you.

A boy makes a man when the time is right,
Ready, alert, and prepared.

This time he was forced to fight,
Outsmarting others when dared.

Moving On

That afternoon, Hardin woke up. He was dirty and hungry. You could buy a hot bath at the rooming house, so he had them heat some water and pour it into the tub in the special room they had for baths. With plenty of soap and hot water, he soon felt clean again. He pulled some clean clothes out of his clothing bag and combed his hair before he went to eat.

Outside, he saw a saloon with food about a block from the rooming house. He seated himself at a table, and a pretty, young girl came over to take his order.

Fifteen-year-old Hardin was handsome. His dark brown hair was combed back to show his strong facial features, and he had a dark tan from being outside in the sun and weather so much. His eyes were of an unusual, deep blue color, and his directness of manner gave the impression of confidence. At five foot ten inches tall, the muscular Hardin had a strong and confident presence, and the other customers noticed it as he pulled up his chair.

The waitress smiled and said that her name was Susie. Their special was meatloaf, mashed potatoes, corn, cornbread, and gravy. He could have apple pie for dessert if he wanted it. That sounded good to Hardin, so he said that he would like all of it, even the pie. As she wrote down the order, she asked Hardin where he was from.

He said, "My name is Hardin Hammond, and I'm riding from Osceola to Quincy to go to school."

"That's a long way, Hardin," she said. "I wish that I could go someplace like that. You have a lot of courage to make the trip alone. If you are going to be in town long, I would be glad to show you around. I get off in a little while."

"I'll be leaving in about an hour, but if you are off from work by then, we could walk down to the stable and talk while I saddle up my horse, Brownie. You would be pleasant company. It gets pretty lonely out on the road," Hardin said.

"After you finish eating, I'll be glad to walk with you," Susie said. Her perfume smelled good to Hardin. It had been quite a while since he had been that close to a pretty girl. She seemed so nice and friendly. He was looking forward to talking with her after his supper.

While he was eating, the sheriff came in to have supper with some friends. They sat within earshot of Hardin. He heard the sheriff telling his friends about how he and his deputies had caught the robbers. There was no mention of Hardin; the sheriff was taking as much credit as he could. Hardin figured the sheriff must have needed the recognition so that the townspeople would have faith in his abilities and respect him. But right now, knowing how the bad men had really been captured, Hardin lost his respect for the sheriff. Clearly, he wasn't honest or truthful.

John Robert had told Hardin that there were two things to keep in mind when he thought that he'd been successful at something. The first was that success was fleeting. The second was that "Success has many fathers, failure only one." Hardin knew that the sheriff was claiming to be the father of his success. He was ready to put Sedalia behind him and move on. If he rode until dark tonight, he could cross the Missouri River at Boonboro by tomorrow evening. He still had a long way to go before he reached Quincy, and he had lost some time that day.

Susie came by his table as he was finishing up his delicious dessert of apple pie. "They let me off early," she said. "I'll walk with you down to the stable. I want to hear more about your trip. Besides, someone needs to see you off."

Hardin picked up his things at the rooming house. They walked on the boardwalk through town as she talked about her life there. She lived with her mother and two sisters. Her father had disappeared several years ago. Susie's income helped the family get by. They had a little house on the edge of town. She walked close to Hardin, her brown eyes looking for hope and compassion in his. Hardin was glad for her pleasant companionship and warm friendliness.

They were at the stable now. Brownie stood still as Hardin fitted him out with saddle, bridle, bedroll and food, and the Henry rifle in its scabbard. Susie watched him as he prepared to ride until dark and bed down for the night. They were both quiet as Hardin felt the inner pull of her friendliness and charm against the loneliness he would face on the road ahead. It would be easy for him to stay another night.

"Susie, thank you so much for seeing me off," Hardin said. "You are a delight, and I only wish that I had more time to spend with you. I think that we will always be friends. But I have to go now and get my schooling—that's what I have set out to do."

Susie's eyes looked misty as they stood there in an awkward silence. Young men like Hardin didn't come by Sedalia very often. He had touched her with his warmth and understanding, and she wanted to know him better. She said, "Don't let anything happen to you, Hardin, and good luck with your schooling. I know that you will be a big success someday."

Susie held his arm and leaned up to kiss his cheek in a lingering and loving way. Hardin could feel her warm body and lips pressed against him.

She said, "Good luck, Hardin, when you come back through, stop and let me know how you are doing."

"I will, Susie," he said. It was time to go. Getting up onto Brownie seemed like the hardest thing Hardin had ever done. He looked back once, and Susie was still standing there and giving him a big wave. Hardin waved back. Brownie steadily walked down the street and out of town.

Hardin could feel Susie's warm kiss on his cheek for a long time. He thought about the possibilities with her as he rode far into the night.

Tempted

When you are tired and lonely
At the tender age of love's bloom,
If you could feel her touch only,
It would sweep away your gloom.

Your senses beg you, stop for a while,
Linger and savor her care,
But duty calls beyond her smile,
Ride on, and soon you'll be there.

Crossing the River

~~~~~~~~~~~~~~~~~

Hardin and Brownie rode down the road away from the town. Soon they were back in the country. The steeper hills of the Ozarks had gradually turned into rolling, flatter land with fields of corn and hay.

As the evening gradually turned to twilight, Hardin could see lamps that had just been lit in the sprinkling of farmhouses he passed. He searched the lighted windows for any signs of human life. He was feeling lonely and wished that he were inside one of those cozy farmhouses, having fun with his brothers and sister, or with someone like Susie, whom he yearned to hold and touch and be close to. But Brownie just kept moving toward Quincy and the school Hardin would attend. It was a responsibility with mixed blessings.

The next morning, Hardin stepped out of his bedroll and saw the sky was clouding up. It looked like a storm was moving in from the west. As he looked at the western sky, he saw that the clouds were growing darker and lower off in the distance. Then the wind changed from west to east. There was a storm coming, and Hardin needed to make sure that his rain gear was handy.

After eating some breakfast, Hardin put the plastic cover over his straw hat. Then he pulled out his plastic raincoat and put it in the top of his saddlebag. He wanted to reach the ferry at Boonville by nightfall so that he could get across the Missouri River before it was too high and dangerous from the storm. He would have to push Brownie down the road today in order to reach the river in time to cross it.

The clouds became darker, and the distant rumble of thunder foretold of a bad thunderstorm making its way toward him. Looking over his left shoulder, he could see jagged bolts of lightning getting closer to him and Brownie. Hardin knew that this was the front of the storm coming through, and then there would be mostly rain with less lightning.

When the storm hit, Hardin pulled Brownie toward the side of a hill, which gave them some protection. The storm was bad, but they were safe as it passed through. After about forty-five minutes, the worst part of the storm had swept on eastward, leaving a steady rain falling in its wake. It didn't look like the rain would let up soon, so Hardin nudged Brownie back onto the road toward Boonville.

That evening, they reached the crossing point at Boonville. There was an old man who ran the ferry, and his son helped with the process of getting horses and people across the Missouri on their raft. The man looked at Hardin and Brownie with some surprise. They were drenched from the constant rain, and both were tired from the hard day.

"It'll cost you three dollars," the river man said. "We have to go soon because the river is coming up from that rain. If we don't cross tonight, you will have to wait three or four days."

"Let's go, then," Hardin said. He paid the man three dollars, and they went down to the ferry.

The ferry was a raft with rails on each side and planked gates at each end. At most, it would haul three horses and riders at a time. There was a large pulley on each side of the river with a heavy rope stretched between a large tree and the raft. The son led a team of mules away from the river to pull the ferry across. He reversed the process to bring it back. The old man had a long pole to help direct the raft when they came in close to shore. It was a scary way to cross, but the man probably knew what he was doing. Hardin led Brownie down onto the raft.

The little horse's legs were shaking on the unstable platform. Hardin held Brownie tight by the rail so that their weight wouldn't shift. The raft bobbed and turned back and forth in the swift water as they moved out into the current. The rain was still pouring down. It was a rough ride.

Finally, they made it to the other side. "I can't make it close to shore because the river is up already. You will have to get out here. The water is waist deep, but you can still make it," said the man, showing Hardin the depth with his pole.

Hardin didn't have any choice. He jumped in and found the mud bottom. The brown river water surrounded him up to his chest. He started toward the riverbank, trying to pull Brownie by the reins, but Brownie wouldn't budge. The man whacked Brownie on the behind with his pole, and Brownie jumped into the water. Hardin fell backwards, but he regained his balance. Finally, Brownie found his footing, and they made it up the riverbank and onto solid ground.

The river man waved as the raft headed back across the river. Hardin knew he would have a lot of cleaning up to do tomorrow. He was especially worried about getting his rifle wet, but he had oil and knew how to clean it.

After pulling the saddle off of Brownie, Hardin found a place in the grass under a tree and went to sleep in his raincoat and wet clothes. He smiled to himself right before he fell asleep. It had been the hardest day yet, but it had been exciting. He and Brownie had made it. By tomorrow, maybe the storm would be past, and then he could clean his rifle and dry his clothes.

He was more than halfway to Quincy, and he was making a journey that he would always treasure. Hardin's confidence in himself was growing rapidly. The trip was good for him, and he was finding that he was as much of a man as anyone.

The Storm

Dark clouds rolled in from the west.
They struggled through rain until night.
The Missouri was rising, the man thought it best
To cross now and give it a fight.

Legs wobbled, hooves slid, Brownie clambered on.
The pitching raft through the waves was a trip.
Hardin grabbed Brownie and they were gone.
Luckily, they made it without a bad slip.

New Friends

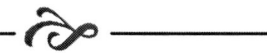

The sounds of a man shouting and cattle mooing woke Hardin up with a start the next morning. It was early, and it was still raining. He was drenched to the skin, and his muscles were aching. He felt like a herd of cows had run all over him. He was hungry and tired and hated to get up, since his wet clothes would only get colder when he moved around. It looked like it would rain all day. There was a layer of clouds as far as the eye could see.

The Missouri River was raging out of its banks only thirty feet away. It had risen during the night, and it was swift and muddy as it flowed by, logs and roots drifting in its boiling waters.

Above the roar of the river, Hardin could hear a man chasing cattle on the ridge. They had apparently escaped and were agitated by the noise and turmoil from the river. "He probably needs some help," Hardin thought to himself. The cattle could go over a cliff if they ran too far in the wrong direction.

Calling to Brownie, Hardin gathered up his wet saddle and bedroll. He threw it up onto Brownie's back, cinched the saddle, and mounted up. Riding up the slippery road in the mud was tough for the little horse, but soon they came to the man and the cattle.

"Need some help?" Hardin loudly asked over the noise of rain and cattle.

"Sure do!" the man said. "These cattle want to go to the river. They got under the fence back home, and I caught up with them here. If you ride over by that big rock on the ridge, I think that we can drive them back to the gate."

Once he was in position, Hardin and the man—who was on foot—drove the cattle back over the ridge and across a field to the man's fenced-in pasture. Together they managed it easily, but one man alone had been not enough to turn the big animals.

"My name's Pete," the man said.

"Hardin," Hardin answered.

As they shook hands, Hardin saw that the man's left arm was missing down below his elbow. The man glanced at what was left of his arm and simply said, "Civil War. A cannonball got me." He smiled as he said it, as if it were nothing. Hardin could see that he got along well despite the loss of it.

"You are drenched," Pete said. "Come up to the house, and we'll have some breakfast. You need to dry those clothes and clean that rifle, too. My wife Amy is cooking right now. I hope you don't mind little kids. My three are a handful on a rainy day like this."

Hardin could see that Pete was around forty years old. He had a short beard that was shaped and a twinkle in his sea-blue eyes, and he was outgoing and friendly. It was good to be with someone who didn't seem "just out to get you or your money" for once.

The house was a three-room cabin built up on the bluff. It had a wide front porch with a roof over it and overlooked the vast Missouri River Valley below. Out back, there was a barn for cattle and horses. This barn was also where Pete stored hay, oats, and corn for the animals. They led Brownie into the barn, gave him some oats and hay, and hung up the saddle, bridle, and bedroll. The horse was tired and hungry and ate voraciously as soon as they put the food out.

At the house, Pete's wife, Amy, looked up from the stove. She was in her apron, and she was a pretty woman with brown hair and a friendly smile.

"Look what I found down by the river," Pete exclaimed. "A slightly drowned man with his horse. Without them, I don't know if I ever would have gotten those cows back in."

Amy smiled and said, "Looks like we have company for the day. What's your name?"

"I'm Hardin Hammond. I don't mean to put you out."

Amy took charge. "We're glad to have you, Hardin. We don't get much company out here, especially on rainy old days. Pete, take Hardin to the bedroom and loan him some dry clothes. Hang up the wet ones by the stove. I'm cooking a good breakfast for you boys. You look like you need it. How does bacon, eggs, and corn meal mush sound?"

"It sounds great to me," Hardin said. "A good, hot meal is just what I need."

"We've got plenty of hot coffee, too," Amy said. "I'll put on a fresh pot."

As the men went into the bedroom, the little kids came out of the other room. Pete and Amy had two boys and a girl. The girl was the oldest at around six years old. The boys looked to be around five and four. They were excited about the company. Hardin could see at a glance that they were a handful. He thought that someday he would have a wife and a family like this. It was obvious that Pete's family was what gave Pete happiness and fulfillment. He loved them, and he was building up a nice home and farm for his family to enjoy.

Hardin felt very lucky to have run into Pete that morning. Just when the day promised to be miserable, it had turned into something just the opposite: a day in a warm cabin with a new friend and his loving family. Hardin wondered about whether this was the act of a higher power protecting and watching over him or just a lucky accident. He would find in his lifetime that there seemed to be too many lucky accidents to be coincidental. He knew that there was something special about his life and his existence that could never be explained by common sense. He was thankful for what had been given to him. The mere wonder of his life was a miracle to him, and it would continue to be as he pursued his dreams and attained each one. He had seen so many of his brothers and sisters die without reason that life was precious to him and a thing to be appreciated.

Pete and his family represented everything that Hardin wanted when he grew older. He was willing to learn and to work hard. He would always seek a better life for himself and hopefully for his family. Hardin knew that a good life was worth the effort.

A breakfast had never tasted as good as the one that Amy cooked for them on that rainy morning. The kids were laughing and having fun. Pete and Amy talked with Hardin about their life up there on the bluff and their hopes and dreams for the future.

As they sat there, Hardin thought of Susie's sweet kiss when he had left Sedalia. Someday he would have a family like Pete and Amy's. Maybe Susie would still be there next spring when he rode back home. It was good knowing how he would like to live someday.

After breakfast, Pete and Hardin took the Henry rifle apart piece by piece and cleaned and oiled it. Then they put it back together. Pete had used a Henry in the army before he was injured. He showed Hardin little tricks to thoroughly clean and oil every part, including the trigger and firing pin assembly. The rifle looked like new when it was done.

Hardin was getting very tired, so they sent him to the back bedroom to sleep while Amy dried his clothes by the stove. Comfortable and snug in the warm bed, he slept through the day until late afternoon. The smell of vegetable soup cooking on the stove mingled with the warmth of the house and covered him as he lay in the warm blankets and savored the moment. Then he got up and joined the family in the front room to talk and joke about the day.

After dinner, they lit the kerosene lamps and sat out in the main room. Amy played the violin. She played some lively tunes that added feelings of joy and celebration to the evening. Hardin asked to see it, then played for them himself.

The kids ran around inside the house playing hide and seek and had a great time showing off for their visitor. Then Pete popped some popcorn, which turned out great. Everyone ate popcorn while they laughed about the kids and talked about their dreams for the future.

The next morning, Hardin got up early and packed his things. Pete and Amy told him where there was a store a few miles away. There he could buy some food and supplies to last him for the rest of his trip to Quincy.

Pete told Hardin to stop and spend the night whenever he came back through. They would be glad to have him stay over again, and Hardin could tell them how his schooling had gone. Hardin thanked Pete and Amy for drying him out and for a great time. The kids hated to see him go, but Hardin mounted up on Brownie, and waving good-bye to his new friends, he rode on down the road toward Quincy.

A Pleasant Surprise

Sometimes strangers make the best friends.
There's an instant connection, we find.
Is it fate, predestination, or similar trends
That tell us we're all of one kind?

A cup of soup, a warm fire, hearty laughter too,
Time without worry, without name,
Friendship is found between me and you,
As we bond together before the flame.

Lillie

Mary Lilla Hogan looked out over the rail of the steamboat and watched the Mississippi River roll by as the boat made its way upstream from St. Louis. The huge paddleboat was taking the fifteen-year-old girl away from her comfortable home in Belleville, Illinois, to attend the Gem City Business College in bustling Quincy, Illinois. Lillie had left home for the first time only yesterday, and she was nervous about how she would like her new school and whether she would fit in with the other students. Her parents thought that it would be best for her to have more of an education. Business knowledge would be helpful to her throughout her lifetime.

Lillie had left many friends behind when she had boarded the paddlewheel boat the previous day. She really wasn't sure that she needed more education. After all, she was engaged to a man from a well-to-do family, and he was in college working on his law degree. She and Mike Barnett were engaged to be married when he graduated in three years. After that, Lillie planned to have children with Mike. Her role in life would be that of his wife and the mother of his children. Mike would be the breadwinner, using his education to support her and their family.

Lillie thought about Mike and their engagement. He was three years older than she was and always dressed well. Some of her friends thought that he was somewhat stuffy, but they all agreed that he was a good catch as far as Lillie's future was concerned. Lillie had been unsure when Mike had proposed marriage to her at her home. He had already asked her father for her hand in marriage, and her father had given Mike his blessing. Lillie's parents encouraged her to accept his proposal, as she would have a sound future. After a day of considering the prospect, she had told Mike yes.

Lillie's thoughts about her engagement were overshadowed by her lingering doubts about whether Mike was the right man for her to marry. He was intelligent and energetic, but he wasn't a warm and caring person toward her. Mike talked about himself and his accomplishments too much, dominating conversations with little regard for what she had to say. He made Lillie feel like a prize he had won at a fair. He didn't treat her like the very special young lady that others had made her feel that she was. He treated her like a possession. He didn't recognize her special attributes, like knowledge and common sense; he only recognized her obvious beauty. Mike just didn't understand her as a woman. But her fate with Mike was set. Whether she would ever love Mike with all her heart, only time would tell.

For now, Lillie went to her small room on the boat and read some more of the book that she had started. She curled up under the covers in her bed and read a few pages. Soon she fell asleep and dreamed of her home and the friends and family she was leaving.

Tomorrow would come soon enough. There would be new places and people with whom to become acquainted. Right now, resting on her bed was her way of preparing herself for the unknown changes in her life that were bound to come.

Young Plans

A woman's future life is planned.
An ideal marriage, and someday teaching.
Over time, perfect plans are canned,
We follow where our hearts are reaching.

Beauty and charm are the bottom line,
But knowledge and caring wins them all.
Perfect plans for our future are fine,
We dumbly follow them until they fall.

Quincy

Hardin rode Brownie across the passenger side of the railroad bridge that crossed the Mississippi River into Quincy, Illinois. The town was bustling with activity. There were steamships and boats tied to the docks, and workers were unloading goods and supplies to be sold in town. There were stores and people everywhere.

Hardin was tired from his trip, so he began looking for the boarding house where John Robert had arranged for a room for him. They had sent his trunk of clothes ahead by railroad, so he thought it should be there waiting for him. The trunk also contained Hardin's violin. He loved music and had played it often at home, working on his technique and enjoying the sweet sounds that came from it. Everything in the town seemed so hectic compared to life in the country. Both Hardin and Brownie were uneasy in their new surroundings.

Finally, Hardin found his boarding house and moved in. He had one room, and it was close to a bathroom with water. The room was small, but his trunk was there. He wasn't sure what he would have done without it.

Hardin found out from the old couple who owned the house that the Gem City Business College was about five blocks away. There was a stable on the edge of town where he could board Brownie. Mr. and Mrs. Schmidt were helpful, but when they told him about their rules, it was obvious that they treated renting the room as business. But Hardin had a place to stay, and he was glad that it was clean and convenient to the school.

Hardin rode to the stable and arranged for Brownie to be fed and exercised regularly. He planned to ride Brownie out into the countryside on the weekends and explore the area.

Now that Brownie was settled, Hardin walked back to his room, cleaned up, and prepared himself for his first day at Gem City Business College. He planned to apply himself and learn as much as possible before going back home next spring.

The next day, Hardin was in a group of about fifty new students. They were split into five groups and given a tour of the two-story brick building in downtown Quincy. Then they were given their books and schedules of classes. Hardin would be taking penmanship, history, business English, salesmanship, personality development, and business arithmetic the first term.

The school had about two hundred students that year. Hardin's classes varied in size from fifteen to thirty students. Hardin was nervous. His hands were sweating. The other students were just a sea of faces on that first day. He wished that he were back on the farm, working with the cattle. He missed his best friend, Frank Hall, and his older brother, J. Belt. The first day flew by. That evening, Hardin studied his lessons.

The history instructor assigned seats alphabetically on the second day. The students were supposed to introduce themselves to the other students seated in front of and behind them as well as the ones to their left and right. As he turned to the left to introduce himself, Hardin realized that a very pretty young woman was sitting there with her hand outstretched toward him.

"I'm Lillie Hogan," she said, taking his rough hand into her own and gently holding it for a moment.

"Hardin Hammond," he said somewhat nervously. He felt the warmth and softness of her hand and could feel something stirring deep inside of him. In the split second that they touched, she had found his heart. Hardin turned his attention toward the instructor, but he was aware of Lillie's close presence throughout the class.

At the end of the class, Hardin dared to take a long look at Lillie while she was talking with a girlfriend and looking the other way. She was somewhat thin but had a healthy and energetic way about her. She was of moderate height—around five foot six—and had reddish-brown hair and blue eyes. Her eyes had a way of focusing directly on the person she was talking with. Her face was very pretty, and her curly hair framed her features. She seemed friendly and smiled often. Hardin could not help but notice her mouth, which hinted of white teeth surrounded by soft and pretty lips. Lillie was a young Irish woman, and Hardin was instantly intrigued by her.

That evening as Hardin studied in his room, his thoughts wandered to the image of Lillie Hogan that he held in his mind. She was so pretty and energetic. Hardin was somewhat shy when it came to girls. He wanted in the worst way to know her better, but he didn't have any idea how to do it. He looked forward to the next day's history class, when he would be in her presence again. Hardin played some music on his violin as he thought about Lillie. Maybe they would get a chance to talk and become acquainted. Hardin felt the spirit and excitement of adventure and promise with Lillie as he drifted off to sleep.

Hardin only exchanged a few words with Lillie during the rest of the week. On Saturday, he took Brownie up on the bluffs of the Mississippi. In some respects, Hardin considered himself a loner, someone who was self-sufficient and content by himself. He had caught a couple of catfish in the river earlier that morning and had some beans and potatoes to cook. With a skillet and pan, Hardin cooked himself a special lunch and enjoyed being out in nature once again. He enjoyed his private day so much that he planned to do this every Saturday while he was in school.

As the sun began to set, Hardin packed up Brownie and rode back to the stable. Spending his free day in this way had allowed him to try to make sense out of everything that was happening to him. He could also think about Lillie Hogan and picture her sitting beside him in history class, and the thought of her gave him strength.

On Sunday morning, students from the business school attended church services, and on Sunday afternoon, a school picnic was held in the city park. The school provided the food and games. There were softball games and sack races to help the students become better acquainted with each other. Hardin stood on the sidelines, watching the more outgoing students having fun. He played games now and then, but usually he was content just to watch the others.

Hardin was watching the softball game when he noticed Lillie standing next to him. "How come you aren't playing, Hardin?" she asked.

"I guess I'm better with cattle and farming than softball," he answered. "I'm just a country boy here in the big city. Where are you from, Lillie?"

"I'm from Belleville; it's near St. Louis. My folks didn't want to send me too far from home."

"Well, I'm from Osceola, Missouri. It's in the foothills of the Ozarks in western Missouri. I'm here because both of my parents are teachers, and they wanted me to have at least a year of business training before I got going in life."

"What do you want to do after you finish?" Lillie asked.

"I hope to teach some, like my parents do, and buy some land to farm. Farming is something that I like and know about. Right now, I'm here with my horse, Brownie. He's boarded in the stable. I don't know anybody here. I'm not sure that I want to stay. I study in my room every night. Saturday I rode up on the bluffs overlooking the city. I cooked my lunch over a campfire and spent the day up there. I guess I just like to spend time in the woods. It suits me better than being in town surrounded by strangers."

"Well, Hardin," Lillie said, taking his hand in hers, "don't worry; you will like school if you give it a chance. By the way, I like to ride horses too. Don't think that I'm just a city girl who doesn't love the countryside. If you want company, why don't we go to dinner sometime? It would be fun, and you can tell me more about your pilgrimages into the woods. I'm on my way home now, Hardin. I'll see you in history class."

As Lillie walked away, Hardin's heart was pounding, and his mind was trying to digest the conversation they'd just had. Her soft touch and her faint smell of lipstick and perfume lingered with him as he pretended to watch the softball game. He smiled and knew that his year in school promised to bring him hope and fulfillment that he had never expected.

Hardin walked through town to check on Brownie. Then he walked back to his room to study and to think about Lillie. She was his inspiration to do well. He looked forward to Monday's classes.

Hardin had promised to write his parents to assure them that he had successfully made the trip and was at school. He sat at his desk on Sunday evening and wrote with the aid of the kerosene lamp in his room.

Dear Mom and Dad,

I made the trip to Quincy, and I am now settled in my room. It is Sunday evening, and I have been in school for a week. Brownie is in the stable here in town, and school is okay so far. I have met a few students that I like, especially a young lady named Lillie.

The countryside is beautiful along the Mississippi River here, and steamboats arrive at the docks almost every day, delivering people and goods. I took Brownie up in the hills on Saturday for his exercise and had lunch on the bluffs overlooking the river. I'm not used to the activity in town, and I enjoyed going to the country for a day.

School is busy; there are about two hundred students. I study every evening and hope to make good grades. I will be glad when this year is over and I can come back home.

I hope that everything is okay there. Write me now and then. I will keep you posted as the year progresses.

Love,
Hardin

Atoms

Somehow, atoms find each other,
They cling together to form all things.
Our body's atoms seek one another,
And when they find them, our heart sings.

We wonder how, across time and space,
They travel through the air.
But when they win their secret race,
We are thrilled that they are there.

The Dinner Date

─────── ❦ ───────

When Hardin asked Lillie to go out to a restaurant for dinner with him the following Saturday, she told him that she was supposed to go home that weekend. She would plan on having dinner with him the Saturday that was coming up in two weeks. They would meet at 5:00 PM and walk to the Red Baron, a modest restaurant that was located down by the river. Hardin was thrilled about their plans and was looking forward to spending the evening with Lillie.

Hardin saw that Lillie was beautiful in her red, satin dress as he came to the door of her room to take her to dinner. Hardin had spruced himself up as much as he could, and his suit coat gave him an adult look that Lillie took notice of right away.

"My, Hardin, don't you look nice!" she said.

"I feel that I am inferior to your beauty. You take my breath away. Shall we go?"

He took her arm, and they walked gaily down the boardwalk to the restaurant. People they passed gave them approving looks and smiles. It was refreshing to see such an attractive young couple laughing and talking as they went out for the evening.

The Red Baron dining room had flowered, red wallpaper and small tables, each with a white tablecloth and a single lit candle. The hostess seated them in a quiet corner with their menus. Hardin ordered a roast beef dinner, and Lillie asked for the fried catfish with coleslaw and a baked potato.

When the waitress had left to put in their order, Hardin pulled a small package out of his pocket and handed it to Lillie. She was surprised when she opened the little, black, velvet box; inside it was a beautiful silver and glass stickpin that she could wear on her dress. Lillie was flattered and somewhat embarrassed by the nice gift from Hardin. She put the pin on the right side of her dress, next to her collar, and her heart opened up to Hardin and his beautiful gesture.

"Thank you, Hardin, for this beautiful pin. It means so much to me. You really shouldn't have done it, you know, but I must admit that I love it."

Hardin was pleased that she liked her gift. He had spent a whole afternoon looking for just the right one. His budget hadn't allowed for anything fancier, but she seemed happy with it, so the effort had been worth it.

Lillie had a worried look on her face. She became quiet, and then she finally began to speak to him again.

"I have something that I want to tell you, Hardin," Lillie said. "I didn't expect to meet someone who I find so interesting and easy to be with when I came here to Quincy. I want you to know that this dinner with you means so very much to me. The problem is, I am betrothed to another man. My parents have encouraged that relationship. The man's name is Mike Barnett, and his family is very well off. Mike is going to law school, so we won't be getting married for three more years. I just wanted to be honest with you from the beginning. I like you and want to be your friend."

Hardin felt crushed and rejected. He should have known that someone as bright and popular as Lillie would have many suitors. He didn't know what to say, so they sat silently for several minutes. Hardin was confused. He loved Lillie, but she had already been promised to another. He needed time to think.

After a long period of silence, Hardin told Lillie about his feelings.

"Thank you for being so honest with me, Lillie; you are a very special person to tell me your future plans like this. You know that the main goal I have in life is success, and my family is not well to do. But you and I can remain friends as long as I am here. We have so much fun together; it would be a shame to lose our relationship. I will enjoy any time that I can spend with you. I hope that you love this man, Lillie, because love should be the basis for any marriage."

"What does love mean to you, Hardin?"

"Some say that love is when your soul finds its counterpart in someone else's. I guess that describes how I feel about you as well as anything. Some people marry for money, some just because they are lonely, some out of friendship, hoping that it will turn into love, and some because of religion. I guess that when I get married, if I ever do, it will be because I've found someone like you who feels the same way about me as I do about her. We are both young now. Our futures are shaped and changed each day that we are alive. Let us see what tomorrow brings. Thank you, Lillie, for being honest with me tonight," Hardin said. "You will never regret it."

They walked back to her room in silence; each was thinking about what had been said and how it would affect their future. It was the beginning of a long and rewarding relationship.

Disappointment

Hardin began his date with Lillie slow,
His heart beating with desire.
Her pretty face in the candle's glow,
Gave perfection to the evening's fire.

Their conversation started in,
As time went on, they found romance.
He thoughtfully gave her a pretty pin,
But her engagement promise broke the trance.

Falling Ill

One Wednesday in January, Hardin woke up in the morning with a bad headache. His attendance had been perfect at Gem City Business College, and he wanted to keep up his record. Anyway, he was sure that he would feel better by the afternoon.

But as the day went on, Hardin just felt sicker and sicker. The aspirin powder that he took didn't have any effect, and now he also felt very sick to his stomach. He barely made it back to his room after class before he vomited. By then he was pretty sure that he had the flu that had been going around. It was a bad one. Several students had died from the serious illness, and many other students were home in bed, trying to survive.

During the night, Hardin developed a high fever and chills. The next day, he lay in bed, missing his classes. He was too sick to eat. The owners of the boarding house didn't normally take care of anyone, so Hardin just lay in bed all day with some drinking water by his side.

On Friday, Hardin was worse, and he sent a note to the school physician. The doctor was busy with other students, but he said he would come by later that afternoon.

Meanwhile, Lillie was wondering where Hardin was. He never missed class, and now he had missed both Thursday and Friday. He hadn't said anything to her about taking a trip or missing school, so she knew that something was wrong. She asked her history professor if he knew why Hardin wasn't there. The professor told her that he had received a note from the school secretary that said Hardin was out with a bad case of the flu.

As soon as class was over, Lillie walked over to the rooming house and asked the owners where Hardin's room was. They told her that it was upstairs to the right. As she walked up the stairs, she met the school physician coming out of Hardin's room.

"How is he?" Lillie asked.

"He's in a bad way," the doctor answered. "High fever and stomach cramps. He hasn't eaten since Wednesday. He needs to drink some liquid or soup to have the energy to get well. I've been seeing some bad cases lately. I have to go right now, but I'll check back on him tomorrow."

"Thank you, doctor," Lillie said. "I'll see if I can help out in the meantime."

When she entered Hardin's room, Lillie realized just how serious the situation was. There was Hardin, pale and flushed from his fever. He tossed around in his bed but appeared to be asleep. Just a pitcher of water sat on the table by his bed. Fear swept through her. She worried that he was so ill that he might not be strong enough to live. The flu had taken the lives of so many people in Quincy. She couldn't lose Hardin; he meant so much to her. She would do whatever she could to help him get well.

Lillie went downstairs and told the owners that she was going to stay and help Hardin. She said that she might need to use the kitchen some, but she would clean up any mess that she created. Then she went to the general store and bought tomato juice, cheese, crackers, chicken noodle soup, and some extra washcloths and towels. She knew that Hardin had to eat to get his strength back.

Back at the rooming house, Lillie soaked three washcloths in cold water. She placed one on Hardin's forehead and the other two on his chest. He was half awake when it was time for his medicine, so she spooned it into his mouth and held the water glass to his lips so that he could drink. She was pleased that he took a few sips of the water before he shook his head to indicate that he didn't want any more.

Lillie sat in the chair in his room and watched and waited. She could see Hardin shaking from the chills. How you could have a fever and chills at the same time had always been a mystery to her. She left the cool washcloth on his forehead but took the other two off of his chest. Then she found an extra blanket and laid it over him. The blanket seemed to help with the chills, and Hardin fell asleep.

At about 1:00 AM, Hardin woke up. He thought at first that he was dreaming. He saw beautiful Lillie seated close to his bed, watching him intently.

"Hi, Lillie, what are you doing here?" he asked.

Lillie had been so worried that she just started to cry. Tears of relief ran down her cheeks. She knew that Hardin was recovering. His recognizing her was a sign that he would be able to get well.

"Oh, I just dropped by for a visit." She laughed, just kidding with him. "How would you like some nice chicken noodle soup and some crackers? I'll go warm it up on the stove. It'll just take a minute."

"That's sounds real good to me. I can't remember the last time that I had something to eat, especially something cooked by an angel."

Lillie helped Hardin eat the soup and crackers and was pleased to see that he drank a whole glass of water.

"How do you feel, Hardin?"

"I feel a much better," he said. "What day is it?"

"This is Saturday morning, Hardin. I'm glad that you are recovering. I need to go back to my dorm now, but I'll stop by tomorrow around noon to make sure that you are all right. Don't go scaring me like this again, okay?"

Lillie kissed Hardin affectionately on the forehead and slowly walked out of the room, waving good-bye.

Hardin lay in bed, warm with love and thankfulness for Lillie. She had come to his rescue when he had needed it most. At that moment, he knew that would throw down his life for her!

"Wonderful Lillie," he thought as he dozed off to sleep.

The Angel

It's tough when you are very sick,
Alone in some strange place.
God has played you a mean trick.
You might be leaving the human race!

Then somehow your love comes by,
To care for you after all.
Sickly and weak, you give a sigh,
God had given your angel a call.

Going Home

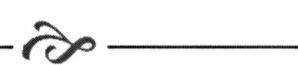

Hardin's final grades were good; he had earned all As and Bs. He had found that he liked to write, and his writing style was clear and evidenced his straightforward thinking. He gave his words a special artistic flair that was rare among his fellow students, and he surprised his teachers with the quality and style of his writing.

Hardin decided to write and tell his parents that he was coming home now. His letter would take about five days to reach his parents in Osceola.

Dear Mom and Dad,

School is finished for the year, and Brownie and I will be starting for home tomorrow. My trunk will be coming by train and will be in Osceola before I get there.

My grades are good, and the year went by faster than I thought that it would. I am anxious to come home now. I like farming and being in the country more than living in the city.

I hope to stop and see some friends that I made close to Boonville. Pete and Amy live with their three children on the river bluff, and I told them that I would stop by on my way back.

I should be home in about one week. I can't wait to tell you all about my experiences.

Love,
Hardin

After shipping his trunk home on the stagecoach, Hardin saddled up Brownie and packed his bedroll and supplies behind the saddle on the back of his faithful horse. His final act of preparation for the trip was to slide his Henry rifle into the scabbard on the right side of the saddle. It would be a long trip, and he wanted to be ready for anything that came along.

Hardin rode Brownie slowly through the streets of Quincy. He turned up the street where Lillie lived; he wanted to see her one last time and say good-bye. At Lillie's rooming house, Hardin stopped and tied Brownie's reins to the hitching rail. Sliding off of the horse, Hardin walked slowly up to her door and knocked.

Lillie came to the door. She knew that Hardin had come to say good-bye. Her deepest fear was that letting him go would be the worst mistake she had ever made in her life.

Lillie now knew that she was in love with Hardin, but she had given her word that she would marry Mike Barnett in two more years. Was Mike really the one for her? She now realized that she had made her choice based upon her parents' and friends' encouragement. She had made her decision based upon security and prosperity, not because of her love for Mike. Now, the man that she had fallen in love with, who had made her so happy with his fun and caring personality, was leaving to go home. At that moment, Lillie felt a loss in her life that she believed could never be filled again.

The look on Lillie's face gave away how sad she felt that Hardin was going across the state to go home. She stood silently in the doorway, feeling his presence. There was a long minute before Hardin broke the silence with his words.

"I'm leaving now, Lillie. My year at Gem City is over, and I'm going back to Osceola to live with my family. I hope to work hard and save my money to buy a farm. That's what I have always wanted to do, and my education here will help me with my plans.

"Lillie, you have been a godsend to me. I hope that you will be my friend forever. I shall never forget your pretty laugh and the fun that we have had this year. I will write you when I get back and tell you how the trip went. Thank you, Lillie, for your friendship and caring. You gave me great comfort while I attended school here. Knowing you was the best part of my year away from home."

Small tears trickled down Lillie's cheeks as she hugged Hardin. Gently, she placed warm kisses on his cheek. "I will miss you, Hardin. You mean more to me than you will ever know. Please take care of yourself and write often. I want to keep in touch always and will write to you too. We will always be friends."

Hardin's heart was pounding as he rode Brownie down the street away from Lillie and left town. He knew that he was in love with Lillie, but she was promised to another man, a man whose prospects for the future were better than anything that Hardin could offer her. Hardin knew that he needed to go home and build his future while living close to his family and friends.

The memory of Lillie's hugs and kisses warmed Hardin as he and Brownie headed down the long trail toward home.

Leaving

It's hard to leave the friends you've found;
Change in life isn't always fair.
You set your sights on familiar ground,
Pack up your horse and leave for there.

But wait; what about the love you feel?
Time ran out, changed everything.
Back down the road you steal,
Feeling the loss, enduring the sting.

Reunion with Friends

A few days later, Hardin reached the Missouri River near Boonville. He was getting lonely from the tedious ride and was finally at Pete and Amy's. It was a visit that he had been anticipating because he had so many stories to tell them about his year in Quincy. As Brownie walked up the road toward the cabin, Pete came to the door.

"Hardin! Welcome! How did you like going to school in Quincy?"

"It was good, Pete. How are you and Amy doing?"

Hardin jumped off of Brownie and ran up to the porch to grab Pete's hand. They went inside, talking and laughing. Hardin said hello to Amy and the kids. It was a joyful reunion. They insisted that Hardin eat supper with them and spend the night. Hardin offered little resistance. He knew that it would be fun to see the family and it would be a good break in his trip.

It was almost as if the year between the two visits hadn't happened. Hardin told Pete and Amy about his plans to have a farm in the future. Pete gave him all of the advice that he could think of, and Hardin listened carefully. He knew that Pete was a good farmer and knew how to raise cattle. Finally, they all called it a night and went to bed. Hardin slept well in the comfortable home of his good friends.

The next day after breakfast, Hardin said good-bye and rode down to the river ferry landing. The ferry ride across the Missouri went smoothly. Starting out on Brownie again, Hardin knew that he would make it to Sedalia by nightfall. He would stay at the hotel and bathe. Then he thought he would have supper in the restaurant and say hi to Susie; he had promised her that he would stop by on his way back.

That evening, a clean and refreshed Hardin walked from the hotel to the restaurant in Sedalia. He wondered how Susie was and still felt the sweetness of their visit when he had seen her last fall. Entering the restaurant, Hardin saw Susie waiting on a table on the far side of the room. It was easily apparent to him that she was with child. "How things can change over a little time," he thought to himself.

Susie recognized him as she came to take his order. "Hi, Hardin, it's good to see you again. How did it go?"

"Hi, Susie. I made it through the year, and now I'm headed for home. How are you?" Hardin asked.

She smiled at him. "As you can see, I'm going to have a baby. I got myself married while you were in school. I'm happy. My husband and I are building a small house on the edge of town."

She took his order: pork chops with stuffing and lima beans. He would have corn bread on the side. He asked for cherry pie for his dessert.

"I'll put this in right away. We're very busy tonight, but I'm glad that you stopped by. If we don't get a chance to talk, it was good seeing you again."

Hardin realized that things had changed now that Susie was married. She looked happy. Hardin felt good that he had found her in good spirits and that she was looking forward to having her baby.

After his hearty dinner, Hardin paid his bill and slipped out of the restaurant. He would get a good night's rest and be home in a few days. He was glad for Susie and happy he had kept his word to stop on his way home. Tomorrow he would move on.

Hardin knew that he had grown and proven himself over the year that he had been gone. Now he planned to use what he had learned to build a good life for himself. He was confident and proud of his accomplishments.

Checking In

It doesn't matter how long it's been
When you stop in to see your friends.
They open their arms like next of kin,
And are glad to discuss the trends.

Good rest, good food, good company too,
Refresh the traveler for his journey back.
They enjoy the time spent with you,
And watch as you ride on down the track.

Building a Future

Five years later, Hardin rode across the wooden bridge over Cooper's Creek and up the winding path that led to Old Baldy. It was 1882, and he was still making his periodic pilgrimages up to the top of the hill to enjoy the peaceful, beautiful scenery of Pleasant Valley as he cooked his lunch over a fire. It was his way of reconnecting with himself and his place in a world that was always changing and challenging him. It was a special time to get in touch with his feelings and evaluate the course he had chosen for himself in life.

Hardin rode a big, black gelding now, having put an aging little Brownie into the pasture with the other horses. Hardin taught school at Chalk Level each day. He worked on building up his livestock holdings in the evenings and on weekends. He had grown a black mustache, which added a strong and handsome look to his features and matched his full eyebrows and close-cropped hair. He still lived with John Robert and Mary Owen, who both taught school as well. Hardin helped them out when they needed him and tended to his growing number of cattle and hogs in the mornings and evenings.

John Robert and Mary Owen had sold Woodland Home and moved to a home on forty acres adjacent to the Pleasant Valley Stock Farm. Their new home was named Fairy Glen Farm. The house was about half a mile from the large house on the Pleasant Valley Stock Farm, which was the farm that Hardin wanted to buy someday. He had proved that he was an excellent judge of the value of livestock, and he was making good money by taking cattle and hogs by railroad to be sold in large city markets. J. Belt and the rest of the family worked together to help him build his herd of cattle on a piece of land he rented in the corner of Pleasant Valley Farm. He was saving his money to buy the farm.

As Hardin cooked his catfish from Cooper's Creek and heated the beans and potatoes that he had brought from home, he thought of Lillie Hogan and how much he missed her. They exchanged letters periodically, and he knew that she wasn't feeling fulfilled in her current situation. Her fiancé, the man she had faithfully waited three years to marry, had fallen in love with a law school classmate and broken off their engagement. Lillie was now teaching school in Collinsville, about eight miles from Belleville, and was still living with her parents.

Hardin worked hard during the week. Saturday nights, he rode with his friend Frank Hall to attend the dances that were held in the large back room of the general store in Monegaw Springs. Hardin played his violin with the small group of musicians who gathered there. Sometimes he met interesting young women. He periodically got involved with someone romantically, but he never had the same feeling of mutual love that had passed between himself and Lillie.

Hardin was dead set on buying Pleasant Valley Stock Farm and building it into a large and prosperous farm. He wasn't ready to settle down and get married; he was more interested in being a success. He was willing to travel a lot, work hard, and take risks to become one. There was a trip to St. Louis coming up; he would sell some cattle at the livestock market there. He was taking them by rail in August.

While he was there, Hardin wanted to see Lillie again. He wanted to find out if their love was still strong. In the back of his mind, he dared to dream for a moment that he would marry Lillie someday. Yes! He would write Lillie and ask if he could call on her on the Sunday that he would be in town. He would go to Belleville, and they could go on a picnic, just like the old days. He could take his violin and play for her, and they could sing their favorite songs together.

Hardin packed his saddlebag with his skillet and pans and rode slowly back down the path. He thought about Lillie as he rode, and his heart raced a bit at the prospect of seeing her again. He would write her a letter that evening. Hopefully, she was not already taken by someone else. Even so, it would do his heart good just see her.

Hardin was in a good mood as he made his way back to the Fairy Glen Farm. He was excited about the prospect of seeing Lillie again. Sweet Lillie, who had watched over him when he was so sick. The thought of Lillie warmed Hardin. He knew that she had always cared about him, and that was a good feeling.

That evening, Hardin wrote to Lillie.

Dear Lillie,

I will be bringing some cattle to St. Louis to market this coming Saturday, August 21. I would like very much to call on you at your home on Sunday. I was thinking that I could pick you up in a buggy and that we could go on a picnic.

If this is acceptable to you, I will come by at 1:00 PM on Sunday and bring sandwiches and some other food with me. I would enjoy your company very much.

It has been too long since we have spent time together, and I find myself missing your interesting conversation and company.

Please write and let me know if this picnic is something that you would like to do.

Sincerely,
Hardin

Ten days later, Lillie's reply came in the mail for Hardin.

Dear Hardin,

It was so good to hear from you. Your letter gave me great cheer, as I have been thinking about you and wondering how you were doing back in your area of Missouri. My life has had its ups and downs since you left Quincy and went home to build your farm.

Lately, I have been taking care of my parents most of the time. They are getting somewhat feeble and need constant attention and care. I am excited to see you again and have one of our special talks. It will be just like the old days.

I will expect you at 1:00 PM on Sunday, August 22 at my parents' home in Belleville. The address is 101 High Street. It is the white, two-story house on the corner.

Thank you for writing and coming to spend the afternoon with me. I am looking forward to seeing you again.

Sincerely,
Lillie

Hardin folded the letter and placed it in his coat pocket. His heart was beating from the excitement that he felt about seeing Lillie. He treasured her reply. To have her written words close to his heart gave him comfort, and he anticipated her gentle and caring presence. Hardin knew that he had never stopped loving Lillie. His hope was that she would still love him too.

Twenty-One

A perfect age, some might say,
Is often lonely too.
Learn and work, grow each day,
Inside wishing for love so true.

There must be more to life,
When missing another's sweet care,
Her gentle touch would quench the strife,
Sweet memories remind me that she's there.

Directions in Life

The miracle of each life lies within the tiny thread of events that leads us down separate paths throughout our lifetimes. Beginning with the actual act of being born, we make our way from childhood into adulthood as we grow through all kinds of dangers. We also meet with unlimited opportunities as we travel through the tenuous existence that we experience here on earth.

Part of our journey is one of tradition. The occupations, values, and habits of our families eventually become the traits that we assume for ourselves. We develop other aspects based on our geographical locations. Were we raised in Alaska, California, or even western Missouri? Climates, cultures, and even the terrain that surrounds us all affect our lives in different ways.

Some people die at an early age. They never have a chance to meet the many challenges that others face throughout their lifetimes. Others live to be ninety or even a hundred years old, having been blessed with good health. Through pure luck, one might escape life-threatening events like mine disasters, lightning strikes, tornadoes, and fatal illnesses that take many lives each day.

Hardin believed that a higher power controlled his destiny. He felt that living a good life included worshipping and being thankful. He hoped to be able to take advantage of the opportunities that would come to him in the future. He remembered well that many of his brothers and sisters had had their lives taken from them at early ages. Out of thirteen children, only four remained. Yes, he believed that he was a special person. His life had been spared so that he could make a difference in his world.

Each day, Hardin made choices and decisions that drove his life in the ways he wished it would go. To him, having a large stock farm and becoming a leader in his community were most important. He knew that he was constantly acquiring knowledge and skills to enhance his career. Because of his extraordinary effort and drive, he knew that he would become successful at a young age. He would do his best to justify his existence on this earth and try to prove that he was deserving of the confidence his higher power had in him. He knew that each day of his life was a gift, and he wanted to return that gift with goodness and use his strength and abilities to make the world a better place. Hardin thought that he had been chosen for that purpose.

He was still considered young at age twenty-one, but each day, Hardin was building a solid reputation as an honest and hard-working man with a good future.

His friend Frank Hall was content to work at Teal Zyler's Bar in Osceola, and his older brother J. Belt just helped out with farming when he was needed. Hardin saw that they had no real futures. They would always be happy with average positions in life.

Hardin wanted to stand out and accomplish something every day. Even when he was practicing his violin or reading in the evenings, Hardin felt the satisfaction of learning, improving, and growing as he pursued his interests.

Now Hardin would soon see Lillie again. He knew from her letters that she was caring for her parents because they were both in poor health. In another year, he would have enough money to buy the house and a part of the Pleasant Valley Stock Farm. The owners had said they would be willing to sell it to him for a fair price.

Would this be the time to talk to Lillie about marriage? Would she leave her parents to move to Osceola? Did she have another fiancé now? Was Hardin truly worthy of her love, or were they destined to always be just friends? Above all, Hardin worried about whether Lillie would find him worthy of being her husband. His palms grew moist with sweat at the fear of being turned down by her. Her beautiful image had been with him since they had first met in Quincy, and he now believed that his happiness depended upon her becoming his partner in life.

The trip to St Louis promised so much, yet Hardin was scared to face its life-changing outcome. His mind was haunted by the memory of the encouraging words in her letter. Would she feel the same love for him that he held in his heart for her? Only Hardin's higher power knew the answer, and his higher power was going to let Hardin find out for himself!

Fate

Fate plays its surprising part
Just when we have given up.
Suddenly, it gives you a start,

And happiness overflows your cup!

It's my higher power, you say,
Maybe luck or chance.
But now on this special day,
Love makes your beating heart dance!

Reuniting with Lillie

Lillie sat on a blanket with Hardin high on the bluff over the Mississippi River. She noticed how he had changed from the boy she had known in Quincy to a confident and handsome young man. Hardin told her about the definite vision he had of his future. He wanted Pleasant Valley Farm, and he wanted success in life.

Lillie marveled at the change in his perception of his life. Somehow, she had not realized that the drive and values that she had recognized in him five years ago would now reveal their strength through his strong looks and bearing. Hardin Hammond was the man that she still loved. Today she saw the strong and worthwhile person that he had become. She hoped that he would still want her as well.

After playing "Beautiful Dreamer" and some more of their favorite songs on his violin, Hardin took Lillie's hand. They sat silently in the twilight. They sat that way for a long time, feeling each other's energy and love through the warmth of each other's hands and bodies.

"Is there any chance that someday you might come to western Missouri and marry me, Lillie?" Hardin softly asked her.

"You know that both my father and my mother are ill and very old. I am the only one left in my family who can care for them. I have that responsibility now, and they must remain in their home because they would not be able to live anywhere else. They have been good to me. I cannot move away from home while they are still alive. I do love you Hardin, but I must put my desires for you on hold while I do my duty."

"I love you too, Lillie. I cannot shake the memory of you no matter where I am or what I am doing. The vision of having you as my wife someday drives me to try my best to succeed in life every single day. You are my dream," he said.

Their lips met in a passionate kiss that left Hardin shaking with desire. They lay on the blanket in each other's embrace as the evening turned to night.

Finally, it was time to go. The young couple reluctantly loaded up the buggy, and Hardin drove the horse-drawn carriage back to Lillie's. He had to let her go that night, and he would regret their parting for several years.

"Sometime in the future, Lillie, we will be together," he promised. Their good-bye kiss was wet with her tears.

The next morning, Hardin was on the train heading back to the Missouri countryside. He was going to the bank with his money to purchase the Pleasant Valley Stock farm.

He vowed to himself that someday he would marry Lillie. She would complete him as no one else could. They would build their future lives on the farm. Hardin knew that he could find happiness with her by his side.

As the train rolled through the countryside, Hardin knew that someday his dream would come true. It would happen when the time was right. Meanwhile, he would give everything he had to become successful.

Responsibility

What of my family, someone said,
When they are old and gray?
Will they be cared for 'til they're dead
Or left alone to pine away?

I need to help them carry on,
They've done so much for me.
And when they are dead and gone,
I'll spend some time with thee.

Taking the Risk

The bankers at the Farmers and Merchants Bank in Osceola looked over their spectacles at the young man seated at the conference table in the bank. The young man's father, John Robert, was there by his side.

Hardin laid all of his cards on the table. He had several thousand dollars, thirty cattle, twenty hogs, and the knowledge that he had acquired while helping Ory Sutter on his farm.

John Robert threw in the final chip. He would sign on the purchase of Pleasant Valley Farm and pledge the assets of Fairy Glen Farm on the loan to guarantee it. John Robert had seen what Hardin could do and knew that he would be successful.

The bankers looked at each other with a serious and cautious demeanor. "You know, Hardin, that if you can't make your payments, the bank will have to take the farm back," the bank president said. "You will lose all of the money and stock that you have built up. If the market goes bad, John Robert could lose his farm, too."

"Dad and I have thought about this. We believe that the farm has great potential. We have no doubt that Pleasant Valley Farm will someday become one of the most prosperous farms in the area. I know that I can do it!"

The bankers knew that the present owners of Pleasant Valley Farm had been letting the property deteriorate for the past several years. Maybe this young man with such drive and enthusiasm could rebuild it. With the money and equity that the Hammonds were putting down on the mortgage, the bank would be secure. If they had to take the farm back, they would still have enough equity left to sell the farms and get back their loan money from the proceeds of the sale. Meanwhile, the interest income would be a huge benefit to the little bank.

The bankers nodded their heads in agreement. They would give Hardin his chance to build up Pleasant Valley Farm. They hoped that he could do it!

The Gamble

*"All life's a gamble,"
The old man grimly said.
"It's chancy as we ramble
And try to get ahead."*

*Some things, they don't work out,
Times can be quite rough.
But I say, "Don't ever doubt!"
Success is better when it's been tough.*

J. Belt

Hardin's older brother had been helping him work on making the Pleasant Valley Stock farm into a profitable operation. J. Belt was a big man. At six foot four and 250 pounds, he could do a lot of work when he felt like it. J. Belt had moved onto the farm with Hardin. He helped with getting groceries and doing other odd projects. His specialty was carpentry, but many nights he was out late drinking and gambling in Osceola. Hardin often had to put projects on hold until J. Belt was ready to work.

Everyone liked J. Belt. He was always laughing and having fun. He had a lot of friends, though most of them were pretty seedy and rough. J. Belt liked to have a good time. He was at every dance in Monegaw and played cards with the local gamblers whenever there was a game.

Helping Hardin was the one thing that J. Belt really cared about. He loved his hard-working younger brother, but he thought that Hardin was a workaholic who should be spending more time having fun. J. Belt displayed a cheerful exterior, but inside he was confused about his life and how to take responsibility for it.

Having fun in life was J. Belt's main way of hiding his own insecurities and self-doubts. He clowned around with friends, but he couldn't understand his quiet, hard-working brother, who seemed driven by the cause of building a better life. He respected Hardin for his drive and knowledge in running the stock farm, but J. Belt was content to just help out. He didn't want all of that responsibility hanging over his head.

"J. Belt, I need your help," Hardin said as he shook the big man's foot under the covers one morning. "We need to drive twenty head of cattle to Osceola and get them on the train that leaves for Kansas City tonight. I need to sell them to bring some money in for the payment on the farm."

J. Belt murmured something, turned over, and went back to sleep. He had come in at dawn. Hardin saw that he would be no help that day. He thought about riding over to his friend Bill Slagle's house to see if Bill and his two boys could help instead. Bill was raising his boys by himself after his wife had died. The boys, Clarence and Charlie, were too young to be of much help, but they would be fun to take along.

Bill often came over and spent the day with Hardin, talking about his life with the boys and how he missed his wife. He was a good man. Hardin and Bill liked to spend time together and discuss life's twists and turns. Bill's boys always added youthful energy and playfulness when they came to Pleasant Valley Farm. Hardin respected Bill for bringing up the boys while working hard on his own farm to make a living.

Hardin saddled up Big Black and trotted the five miles to Bill's house. It looked as if they had gone to town; the wagon was gone, and no one was home. Next Hardin headed to Frank Hall's farm, which was just a couple of miles farther down the road. Hardin tied Big Black at the gate, walked around to the back porch, and knocked on the door.

Frank was just getting up, and he said he would help Hardin. He told his wife and kids good-bye, and the men rode off together to gather up the cattle. Frank knew that Hardin would pay him something for his help. He was glad to get out of the house that day anyway.

The November weather was cold with a biting wind that carried snowflakes. The men rounded up the cattle and drove them down the road to the train car in Osceola. Frank rode ahead and stopped traffic at the bridge. Then he and Hardin drove the cattle over the Osage and down a side street to the boxcar. Finally, they shouted, pushed, and pried the cattle into the car. Later, Hardin would ride in the passenger car to Kansas City and stay the night. He would see that the cattle were sold for a good price. After selling the cattle, he would take the train back home.

Hardin put Big Black up in the stable in Osceola and saw that he was fed and watered. Then he and Frank went to the restaurant in town and had dinner.

"Thanks, Frank," Hardin said as Frank rode off to go back home. "I'll stop by when I get back and pay you for helping. I couldn't have made it without you."

"No problem, Hardin," Frank said. "It was fun, and I had a good day. I'll see you when you get back."

There were a lot of challenges involved in building the value and appearance of Pleasant Valley Stock Farm, but Hardin didn't mind. He loved working outside with the animals and took pride in keeping his growing herd healthy. His daily hard work and successes gave Hardin satisfaction and a feeling of worthiness that could not be earned any other way.

It was late, and J. Belt was just getting up out of bed again. He felt guilty about not being there when Hardin had needed him. "Oh well," he thought, "Hardin probably got Frank to help him."

J. Belt wished that he were a better person. He just liked to have fun too much.

Brothers

Brothers bond with love so rare,
And together find life's call.
With our brother we always share
The finest gift of all.

They often come on the run,
And hearken to our side,
Ever there, when life's no fun,
Shielding us from life's hurtful tide.

The Farm

After owning the farm for the first five years, Hardin and J. Belt had made many improvements to the house and outbuildings. They had also hired other men from the area to help fix the house up the way Hardin wanted it.

Hardin had taken a partner in his stock trading business named Rufus Parks. Rufus rode through the country with Hardin, buying up hogs and cattle from local farmers. Then they transported them back to Hardin's farm for fattening. When the livestock were ready, they shipped them by railroad to Chicago, St. Louis, or Kansas City to get the highest prices.

Hardin was making a lot of money. He had already added one adjoining farm to Pleasant Valley and was negotiating for another addition. Hardin was known in the area as one of its most successful businessmen. He demonstrated honesty, hard work, and excellent judgment when it came to valuing livestock.

The house at Pleasant Valley Farm was far above average. It was one of the few houses in the area with running water. Two large windmills pumped water to the water tower they had built, which served the house and barn lot. The large yard had many flowers, maple trees, a water hydrant, and a white board fence across the front.

There were ten large rooms besides the bathroom and two porches. The two large rooms that people entered first were called double parlors. They each had beautiful hanging chandeliers and bay windows with colored windows at the tops. There were two separate large bedrooms upstairs. The house was made for a large family. The door to Hardin's farmhouse was always open so that friends and relatives could come and stay with him periodically. They would often help with the farm work when they could.

The outbuildings included a large, red barn with the words "Pleasant Valley Stock Farm" painted in large, white letters on the side facing the road. Out back there were several sheds, granaries, and the important smokehouse where the butchered meat was stored.

The farm was located three fourths of a mile from Pleasant Valley School, three miles from Kidd's Chapel (a large, stone church), three and a half miles from the Chalk Level Store, two and a half miles from the Concord Baptist Church, and about seven miles from both Osceola and Lowry City. It was a pleasant country community where everyone knew each other well.

The farm had grown to 450 acres, and Hardin needed to purchase two other small farms to achieve his goal of owning 700 acres. He could rent the other three farmhouses on the adjoining properties once he had purchased all of them. Then his holdings would be profitable.

When he became more widely known for his success, Hardin was asked to join the board of directors of the Farmers and Merchants Bank in Osceola. This was a high honor, and Hardin accepted the position, knowing that it was a great opportunity for him to learn more about business.

Later that year, Hardin was also asked if he would have the time and interest to serve on the city council of Lowry City. He was honored to be asked, and he joined. He realized that it was important for local leaders to accept the responsibility of making decisions that would improve their community.

Hardin's dreams were coming true, but he wished that he had a family with whom to share his dreams. He had been working so hard on the farm that he had almost forgotten what family life was like. Someday, he wanted to have a wife and children to come home to. Hardin was still young and ambitious. When the time was right, he would get married. He often thought of Lillie and his love for her. She was the one who would be his ideal partner in life. He was secretly hopeful that someday they would be together. But distance and circumstances made his dream of having a life with Lillie difficult to achieve.

First Hardin wanted to build up his farm. He loved the thrill of a good business deal and the excitement of seeing his holdings grow. He loved to walk around his land and watch its progress. A family would make his life complete.

Goals

Work hard and make your goal,
Don't rest too long each day.
Material things brighten your soul,
Live the myth; it's better that way.

That's how life's progress shows,

Its value false and true.
More is better, everyone knows,
But not always fulfilling for you.

The Slagle Boys

One morning, a rider came to the farm with some bad news. Bill Slagle had been shot and killed in a fight in Osceola the night before. The boys, Clarence and Charlie, were nine and eleven years old. They had no other known relatives. There was going to be a community meeting at the Baptist Church that evening to figure out what should be done with the boys.

It upset Hardin that his friend Bill was suddenly gone. When Bill had helped Hardin on the farm, the boys had always been with him. They were good kids and always helped out when they could. He hoped that some family would take them in, but he couldn't think of anyone who could.

Hardin and John Robert went to the meeting. Hardin hoped that the farmers in the community wouldn't send the boys to the orphanage in Clinton; that was the last place Bill would have wanted them to be. The orphanage barely had enough money to operate, and the living conditions were terrible. Hardin and his dad needed to be at the meeting to make sure that the Slagle boys were placed in a good home.

Bossy Mrs. Jones took over as chairwoman of the meeting at the church. Mrs. Jones was a tough old lady. She had lived near Pleasant Valley all of her life and often took charge when decisions had to be made. Since the matter involved young boys, the women in the community wanted to be in on any decision the community made. There were about fifteen concerned neighbors who had come to find out more details about Bill's death. They also wanted to see what would happen to the boys.

Hardin sat in the corner of the room with his hat pulled down on his forehead. John Robert sat closer to the front of the room. Mrs. Jones went on and on about the terrible tragedy. She worried about the two boys who were now alone and cried about poor Bill, whose life had been snuffed out in its prime. There had been a duel in the street because of an argument over cards. Bill had never had a chance, as his murderer was known to be a crack shot. He was one of the bad men about town. The sheriff wouldn't be able to do anything about the killing. It had been a duel and appeared to be fair and square, though everyone had known what the outcome would be.

"Now, is there anyone here who can take these poor boys into their family and raise them as their own?" Mrs. Jones loudly asked. The silence in the room and the hanging of heads clearly indicated that no one was willing or able to take on the responsibility of supporting Clarence and Charlie.

"I hate to say it, then, but I'm afraid they will have to be sent to the orphanage in Clinton," she said.

Hardin felt his stomach tighten up. Sending those boys to Clinton was the kiss of death as far as he was concerned. It wasn't right. The Clinton Orphanage was the former insane asylum, which had been shut down several years ago. Children of various ages stayed there when there was nowhere else for them to go. Several children died at the orphanage each year because of the poor food and living conditions.

Hardin caught the eye of John Robert, who had looked back at him the moment the subject of Clinton came up. Their eyes met as only those of a father and son can, and they made a silent agreement. They both knew something had to be done to save the Slagle boys from the Clinton Orphanage. It had to be done right now, before the final decision was made.

"I'll take them," Hardin said loudly. Every head turned and looked at the young man sitting in the back corner of the room. "They can live with me. I've got plenty of room, and the boys can help around the farm. Bill was my friend. He would want them with me. When I'm on the road, J. Belt and John Robert can keep an eye on them. It looks like I'll need a housekeeper anyway; J. Belt isn't much help in that area." Everyone in the room laughed at that truth.

"Does anyone object to the Slagle boys moving in with Hardin Hammond on Pleasant Valley Farm?" Mrs. Jones asked in a loud voice. No one answered.

"So it's settled," said Mrs. Jones. "Thank you, Hardin, for stepping up to the plate when we needed it most. I'm sure that we all will give you some help with them if you need it. I'll deliver the boys to your house tomorrow morning and help you get them moved in."

"We'll put them in the upstairs bedroom," Hardin said. "It's big, and they can have their own space. Thank you, Mrs. Jones. You did a fine job taking charge of this situation. I'll see that the boys get their schooling and have a home. Sometimes we all have to help each other. I'm glad to do my part."

After the meeting, each member of the committee personally came over and thanked Hardin for his kind act of generosity and compassion. It was clear that

Hardin had acted out of his love for the boys and for humanity in general. He had taken on the responsibility where others could not. Hardin Hammond was someone you could count on when lives were at stake. Everyone deeply respected the person Hardin had become.

The next day, Clarence and Charlie moved to Pleasant Valley Stock Farm. They had their own comfortable room upstairs, and it would be a good place for them to live. They had a lot of healing to do after losing their father. Hardin and J. Belt let them know right away that they were now a part of their family and would never have to worry about being moved again.

Friendship

Does friendship end when life turns,
Taking a back seat to fear?
When responsibility calls with its burns,
Do you chance saving someone dear?

Cross the line in the future we trust,
Our good deeds will pay off some day.
Break the ice that's under your crust,
Help your friend that's now gone away.

Changing Times

The letter came from Lillie Hogan in early September, 1888. Hardin hadn't heard from her for about six months. He knew from her last letter that her mother had passed away and that her father's health was failing. This new letter carried with it the faint scent of Lillie's perfume and was written in her flawless penmanship. It carried a message that would change Hardin's life forever.

My dearest Hardin,

I hope that you are well and taking care of yourself. Life can be so hard, and my thoughts are with you as you work to establish your farm. As for myself, I find that my circumstances are changing.

My father passed to a higher place last July 10. I have been winding up his affairs and have chosen not to teach school in Collinsville this fall. I feel like I need to reevaluate my life. I am considering moving to California. There are a lot of opportunities out there, and my dear cousin says that I can stay with her in San Francisco. I am planning to make the trip next spring. The winter will be too harsh for traveling.

My love for you will be in my heart always. Unfortunately, fate and circumstances often determine the paths we follow in life. I only hope that you will write and that our friendship will last forever.

I must end my letter for now, but I will write again.

As always, my love,
Lillie

Hardin read the letter several times. He was upset and disappointed that Lillie was moving to California. He was twenty-eight years old, and she was twenty-seven. His silent hopes of a family with her were abruptly ending. He had to think. He couldn't lose her. He just couldn't!

Hardin saddled up Big Black, packed his lunch, and rode across the wooden bridge over Cooper's Creek. He turned off of the road and slowly walked Big Black up the trail to the top of Old Baldy. Once his small fire was started, he put his lunch in the skillet, letting it simmer slowly as he sat on the log he had used as his chair so many times before.

Hardin felt sick at heart. Lillie was the only woman he had ever loved, and now she would be leaving. He was very successful in life, but he was so unhappy right now. John Robert had said, "Follow your instincts, Hardin, and go with your feelings." Hardin knew deep down what he had to do. It was time.

He ate his lunch thoughtfully as he planned the letter that he would send back to Lillie. It was an important message that he must draft carefully. He would ask her to marry him and move to Pleasant Valley. If she would have him, he would be the happiest man ever.

Hardin rode back down the hill, excited and worried at the same time. The fear of being rejected by her mixed with thoughts of how happy their lives together could be on the farm. He daydreamed about the family they would raise and the fun that they would have someday.

Maybe he should just hop a train and go there. No! He would write to her first, then go to her if she desired. If her reply was favorable, he would travel to Collinsville soon. The risk of his bold move made his heart pound and made him excited for the future. He wrote her as soon as he got to the house.

My dearest Lillie,

I received your letter today. I wish to extend my condolences to you for the recent loss of your dear father. I know how much he meant to you. You were his angel of mercy. Your unselfishness will be rewarded when you join him in heaven up yonder some day.

I hope that you know that I have always loved you. Your reluctance to marry me and move to Pleasant Valley Farm over the years has been partly due to your dedication to your parents. It was also because I wanted to build a farm that would be suitable for you. Those two deterrents have now been eliminated.

I wish for you to know of my utmost desire.

There are two roads for you to take now. The first road leads to California. I know that you want to start a new life. I'm sure that there are opportunities for you out there, and I know how extremely capable you are. It must be exciting for you to be planning to move into a new world with all of its wonders and surprises.

The second road is the one that I would prefer. If you should fail to choose it, I will be heartbroken, but I will understand and respect your choice.

The second road is to marry me and join me on Pleasant Valley Farm as my wife. We would have children, and your presence would complete my home and my life. Missouri isn't California, but we would make a good life here with you running the household.

If you choose the second road—which I offer with all of my heart—I will come to Belleville to marry you, and we can return with your belongings to Pleasant Valley to begin our lives together.

Please write soon. I pray that your answer will be yes. I would be honored and humbled if you should accept my offer and become Mrs. Hardin Hammond.

I love you and await your reply. If it should be yes, then I will be the happiest man I know.

Affectionately yours,
Hardin

Hardin sealed the letter in an envelope, mounted his horse, and rode to the Osceola post office to make sure that Lillie would receive his message as soon as possible. He wanted her to know of his offer of marriage before she made the arrangements for her California trip.

Hardin knew that it would be at least two weeks before he would receive her reply. He hoped that he had chosen well by sending his letter rather than going to her immediately. Yes, he thought so. The letter would give her time to make her decision clearly and thoughtfully. His fear was that she would say no. His hope was that she would say yes.

Hardin rode back to the farm with emotions raging within him. It would be a stressful two weeks, but he would throw himself into his work and wait for her reply.

If her reply was yes, it would change his life forever.

It's Time

The time is finally right,
Hope comes true at last.
Her letter gave you a fright,
But memories bring back the past.

She loves you, this you know,
Her heart is what you need.
Go to her and clearly show
Your intentions are true indeed.

Joyous Love

When the letter finally came, Hardin's heart was pounding as he wondered about the answer that lay inside the small, white envelope. As he took out his pocket-knife to break the seal, he noticed a faint redness, a light blush, which told of the kiss she had planted on the seal of the letter to carry her love on its important journey. Hardin removed the letter and unfolded it carefully, as if to protect its precious message from any danger. His hands shook slightly as he held the paper and read her reply.

My dearest Hardin,

Your kind letter touched my heart in so many ways. I know that I have always loved you since we first met in Quincy. You are an honorable and ambitious man, yet I see the side of you that is still a boy seeking love and companionship to fulfill his dreams. You want the joy of raising a family with a beloved partner.

I see the side of you that loves to play his violin for friends, to have fun with his wife and children in the evening, and who needs someone to come home to. You need someone who loves you and desires to raise your children. You need a woman to manage your household while you are off working hard to meet your family's needs.

I am overjoyed that you would have me as your wife, Hardin. My answer is a resounding YES! I will spend the rest of my life with you. Our marriage will truly fill the missing part of my life. I was afraid that my dreams of a happy marriage would never be fulfilled.

If you can come to me here in Belleville, we can plan our wedding together. I want so much to see you.

My sisters are already making suggestions, and I will need time to wind up my affairs here. Who knows when I will be making a trip back to this area?

I would like to be married in our family's Baptist church, which we have attended for many years. It is in Collinsville, and they have an opening on Sunday afternoon, January 10, 1889. If this date is suitable for you, it would allow me to spend one last holiday season with my family and friends here and also to wind up my affairs.

Just think: after the wedding, I shall be yours always.

Do come soon!

All of my love,
Lillie

Harden was overjoyed at her acceptance. He knew he had to go to her as soon as possible, so he wrote back that day and rode to Osceola to speed his letter back.

My dearest Lillie,

My heart is overjoyed now that you have accepted my proposal. I can't express to you how happy the prospect of spending my lifetime with you makes me feel.

I will take the train to St. Louis this coming Friday and rent a room near your home in Belleville. Please expect me on Saturday morning at 10:00 AM. We can talk and plan out our marriage and our honeymoon. I will stay on through Sunday so that I can attend church with you and meet your minister.

January 10 is a good date for my family and me. This will give me some time to prepare for your arrival as my bride.

I love you and cannot wait to see you next week!

Love,
Hardin

After posting his letter, he rode back and went over to tell John Robert and Mary Owen the news. They were happy and excited for him, and they all talked of the life that he would enjoy with Lillie on the farm.

The Letter

Grandfather Hardin almost lost
The one he loved the best.
He finally asked her at all cost,
Seeking to settle his quest.

The wait for her reply was long,
He didn't know what to do.
Her letter came with love strong,
It brought thrills to his soul so true.

New Life on the Farm

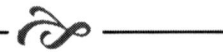

After the fun and excitement of the wedding and a brief honeymoon in St. Louis, Hardin brought Lillie's trunks full of clothes, some furniture, and her other personal items back by rail and buggy to the farm.

It was late January when they arrived, and there were several inches of snow on the ground. A cold wind was blowing from the northwest. As they wound around the hills from Osceola to Pleasant Valley, Lillie thought that the countryside seemed harsh and desolate. Compared to her life in Belleville, which was well populated and a short distance from the bustling city of St. Louis, St. Clair County was wild and untamed.

As the buggy pulled into the entrance of the farm, Lillie saw for the first time the large, attractive house flanked by numerous barns and outbuildings. Hardin was proud to show her the two windmills and the water tank that gave the home running water in the kitchen and the bathroom. Lillie had running water in Belleville, so it was a good thing that it was available to her on the Pleasant Valley Farm.

Inside the house, Lillie entered the two large double parlors where they would receive their guests. The members of the household all came into the parlors to greet her. She was introduced to the Slagle boys, Clarence and Charlie. They had lived there about a year, and they were very helpful and polite. They idolized Hardin, and he treated them as his own boys. They had become very much a part of the family. The boys were ten and twelve years old now and were good about feeding the livestock and helping with the crops. They attended the Pleasant Valley School, which was less than one mile away.

Good-natured J. Belt smiled and laughed when he met Lillie. He went right to work carrying in her bags and trunks and putting them in the bedroom closet. J. Belt was happy for Hardin. He wanted Lillie to be as comfortable as possible, and he hoped to become her friend.

Miss Emmy was the housekeeper. She was a short and wiry woman who was in her forties. She had a very pleasant way about her. She had lived on the farm for the past two years, cooking and cleaning, keeping up the house, and doing chores when necessary. Miss Emmy received Lillie, the new head of the household, with a smile. They would become good friends as time went on.

Miss Emmy had prepared a nice ham dinner with potatoes, squash, and black-eyed peas for Lillie's first dinner at the farm. She had also made two apple pies for dessert. They would eat in a few hours, as Hardin and Lillie had arrived in the late afternoon. Lillie needed time to get settled and arrange her necessary things before dinner.

Hardin took Lillie on a tour of the farmhouse, showing her their master bedroom and bathroom, the many rooms in the house, and the kitchen with its wood cookstove and running water in the sink. There were cabinets stocked with canned fruits and vegetables, cornmeal, flour, and other food that had been harvested last summer.

There was a cellar under the back of the farmhouse that you entered by going through a door and down some steps. Potatoes, beets, apples, pears, and other vegetables would keep long into the winter stored down in the cellar. The earth around the cellar kept the temperature cool throughout the winter and summer.

They also had an icebox, which always had block ice in its bottom section to keep food cold. Hardin explained that smoked meats—ham, beef, and venison—hung in the smokehouse out in the back of the house. Two chicken houses full of chickens provided eggs, which supplemented their diet very well. They also had two milk cows and ten horses on the farm.

Lillie could see that the large farm was very well organized and established. Still, she realized that her life had taken an abrupt change. She would need to use all of her resources as she became the head of the household at Pleasant Valley Farm.

For now, the fires in the stoves and fireplaces gave a pleasant warmth to the lovely home The dinner that Miss Emmy served that evening was delicious, and coffee and pie topped if off. After dinner, Hardin played his violin for the family in the parlor. The warm fire gave them comfort as they enjoyed the winter evening.

The next day was Sunday. Hardin and Lillie attended the Baptist church in the morning. Hardin's brother Claude, his sister Ada, his parents, and several of his friends came to the farm in the afternoon to meet and become acquainted with Lillie.

Claude's and Ada's children played with the other kids out in the yard. Eventually, Miss Emmy brought out fried chicken, potato salad, and vegetables, and they all ate together on the large table in the dining room.

The Pleasant Valley Farm House

Lillie was nervous, as she wanted to be accepted by the family. She was excited by all of the new things that she would have to learn about running a farm. She was becoming a part of Hardin's life, and it brought her the inner peace and happiness that had always seemed to escape her before.

Lillie soon became Hardin's reason for being, and he worked hard on the farm to show her how much he loved her. The Pleasant Valley Farm had found new life, even in the dead of winter.

Family

Lillie married Hardin there,
Her life was dedicated to him.
Meeting the family gave her a scare,
But soon her fears were dim.

Their smiles and friendship so sincere
With simple country charm
Gave her feelings warm comfort here,
She found her home right on the farm.

Adjusting to Farming

During the next three months, Lillie discovered that operating a large farm was often challenging. Everyone had to work as a team to keep the animals healthy, put food on the table, and wash and sew all of the clothes. They also had to run errands to Chalk Level, Osceola, and Lowry City, depending upon what the household needed. Lillie had been a schoolteacher up until then. She found the physical labor on the farm challenging to keep up with. She had to manage her strength for the hard daily work. It was a different lifestyle for her, and adjusting to it would take time.

Hardin woke up very early every morning. He, the Slagle boys, and J. Belt dressed and tended to the livestock before breakfast. The boys milked and fed the cows and tended to the horses. They fed the horses oats with molasses mixed in, and then they gave them hay from the hayloft in the barn. The cows also fed on hay while they were being milked. Some milk was always set aside for the cats that lived in the barn. They would gather around the boys as they milked, waiting for their breakfast. When the cats got too close, the boys squirted them in the face with the milk. They loved to lick the milk off of their faces and whiskers.

Hardin and J. Belt checked on the herd of cattle and the pigs in the hog lot every morning. They carefully looked over each herd, checking for pregnant animals and making sure that the cattle had enough hay and that the pigs had enough corn. It was important to check on the animals' health each day. The livestock represented the wealth of the farm.

By 7:00 AM, the boys and men would come into the house. They would take off their heavy coats and boots and wash up. Lillie and Miss Emmy always prepared a big breakfast. Ham or bacon, eggs, toast, and potatoes was the usual fare. Sometimes they would supplement it with fried cornmeal mush or pancakes. Everyone always ate a big breakfast to prepare for the long day.

Charlie and Clarence Slagle left for Pleasant Valley School by 8:00 AM. They usually walked unless the weather was too bad. If it was storming, J. Belt or Hardin drove them to school in the wagon.

Hardin was usually gone for most of the day. He took care to dress in a suit and wear his black, "Missouri-style," broad-brimmed hat. He would either saddle up Big Black or hitch up the buckboard wagon and head out. He and his partner, Rufus Parks, would ride to local towns and farms and make contracts for calves and piglets that would be delivered later in the spring and summer. Both Hardin and Rufus were excellent judges of livestock and its value.

Hardin came home by nightfall if he wasn't on one of his railroad trips. He worked hard and was often worn out after traveling so much during the day. The family usually turned in about 9:00 PM. The peace and quiet of the countryside lulled their tired and weary minds as they fell asleep.

Saturdays were often fun; everyone would dress up, climb into the carriage, and go to Osceola for groceries. They would also shop for clothing and other useful items. It was a good time to talk with their neighbors and learn about the local gossip. Lillie always looked forward to her Saturday trips to town.

It was the custom to limit farm work as much as possible on Sundays. Everyone would get all cleaned up and attend the Concord Baptist Church on Sunday mornings. The church was located in an attractive and peaceful setting on a hill about two and a half miles away from the farm. The Concord Cemetery was located next to the church, and many deceased local residents were buried there.

Sunday afternoon was the time for family gatherings, usually at Pleasant Valley Farm. Relatives and friends would bring food for a potluck. The women would organize and set up a big meal for everyone who came. In this way, family ties were renewed. Cousins and other neighborhood children played together, and the ladies became better acquainted and discussed subjects that were important to them. Sunday was the day of the week that Lillie enjoyed the most.

Winter turned into springtime, and the rain and the mud that came with it were problems. The men wore knee-high rubber boots as they went out into the feedlots and worked with the animals. Buggies and wagons got stuck on the roads periodically, as the ruts were bad at that time of the year. But after many weeks of hardship, the new life of spring brought hope for the future. Now there were gardens and fields to be planted, and the calf and piglet birthing season began. There was always work to be done, but complaints were scarce, as each person knew that this way of life was good.

In April, Lillie discovered that she was pregnant with their first child. She and Hardin were going to have a family of their own. Both she and Hardin were delighted and excited about the coming birth of their first baby. The child was due the following December.

Lillie had become an important part of the farm and of Hardin's life. He was overjoyed by the prospects for his future. Everything was as he had always hoped it would be. Hardin experienced a deep sense of satisfaction when he returned home in the evenings to Lillie and the farm. They were his pride and joy.

Farm Life

Pleasant Valley Farm prospered
With hard work from them all.
Hardin was building a large herd,
The Slagle boys were growing tall.

Saturday nights they gathered round,
Music and happiness filled the air.
Her piano played with such sweet sound
While his violin sang to her there.

The Hot Summer

In July of 1889, the summer in St. Clair County lived up to its reputation for being hot and sultry. The men were out in the fields each day with the crops and animals. They harvested wheat during the first week of July, then harvested the wheat straw by pitching it onto the big, flat wagon that was pulled by a team of horses. Finally, they pitched it into the barn loft, where it would keep.

The men got three cuttings of hay that summer. It was hot and dusty work. In the fields, they piled the hay so that water would run off of it when it rained or snowed later in the year. The cattle could eat it during the winter to survive. The hay in the barn loft was to be used for the horses and cows in the feedlot. It was handy for them when they stayed in the barn.

The family grew lots of corn—nearly eighty acres of it. It would be used primarily to feed the animals, but some of it would also be ground into meal to be used in household cooking. Cornmeal mush, cornmeal muffins, and the crusty coating on the fried fish they often ate were all made from cornmeal.

The yield from the large garden and orchard kept the women busy in the kitchen canning beans, sweet corn, tomatoes, apples, pears, and other foods. It was hot work, and on hot days, Lillie and Miss Emmy were often drenched in sweat from early morning to late afternoon. They both looked forward to Sundays, when they could renew their faith and energy and visit with their friends and family.

J. Belt was always willing to pitch in when there was hard fieldwork to be done, but he also spent many nights in town drinking and carousing with his friends. Lillie noticed that J. Belt seemed to have a sad side hidden behind his cheerful veneer, but she wasn't sure where his unhappiness came from. She knew that he idolized his younger brother Hardin for his success in business. But J. Belt was fun to be around with his jokes and laughter, and he would do anything to help Lillie out when he wasn't off partying.

Of course, at thirty-two years old, J. Belt should have had a family of his own, but he seemed to be content to live at the farm as part of Hardin's family. Lillie hoped for J. Belt's sake that he would eventually fall in love and settle down, but at this point everyone was glad to have his help on the farm.

John Robert and Mary Owen always came over on Sundays to be with the family. They both still taught school. John Robert was now fifty-three, and Mary Owen was forty-nine. Mary Owen had given birth to thirteen children, nine of whom had died. The two of them had lived through the Civil War, and they had endured a hard life over the years.

Lillie was thankful for the speed at which John Robert and Mary Owen accepted her into the family. Mary Owen was very thoughtful and tried to give Lillie all of the help that she could during her daughter-in-law's pregnancy.

Ada and Claude, Hardin's sister and brother, were both married and had children of their own. They had both moved to the town of Clinton, which was twenty miles away. They mostly came on holidays, when they had the time to make the trip in their buggies.

Lillie struggled with her pregnancy during the hot and humid summer months. But when September came, the air cooled, and she felt much better. It seemed like it was taking forever for the baby to come, and Lillie wasn't a physically strong woman. The others watched over her and helped with the housework so that she would be at her strongest for the delivery.

On December 18, 1889, Lillie's first baby was born. It was a pretty, little baby girl named Edna. She was as cute as a button. Dr. Stratton came from Lowry City for the delivery. He was their family doctor, and he watched over the health of Hardin's family.

Hardin was very excited about their new baby. They all knew it would be a joyous Christmas at Pleasant Valley Farm that year. Claude and Ada came with their children, and they planned a big family party for Christmas Day. They set up tables in the double parlors, and everyone enjoyed the sumptuous feast and lighthearted companionship.

John Robert often liked to perform and entertain everyone at family functions. He had committed several poems to memory, and he would deliver them to family and friends for their pleasure when they all gathered together.

"Everyone get comfortable; go to the bathroom, do whatever else you have to do," Mary Owen said. "John Robert is going to recite one of his favorite poems for you in a few minutes. It's fairly long, but I know that you will like his rendition of 'Lasca.'"

Soon everyone was settled on their chairs and couches, and John Robert stood in front of them. He was dapper in his white shirt and dark suspenders, a true teacher for life. "This is my favorite poem, passed down through generations from Texas," he said. "I hope that you enjoy it."

Then he began reciting with an animated and clear voice.

"'Lasca'

"I want free life and I want fresh air;
And I sigh for the canter after the cattle,
The crack of the whip like shots in a battle,
The medley of horns and hoofs and heads,
That wars and wrangles and scatters and spreads;
The green beneath and the blue above,
And dash and danger, and life and love—
And Lasca!

"Lasca used to ride
On a mouse-gray mustang close by my side,
With blue serape and bright bellied spur;
I laughed with joy as I looked at her!
Little knew she of books or of creeds;
An Ave Maria sufficed her needs;
Little she cared, save to be by my side,
To ride with me, and ever ride,
From San Saba's shore to LaVaca's tide.

"She was bold as the billows that beat,
She was as wild as the breezes that blow;
From her little head to her little feet
She was swayed in her suppleness to and fro
By each gust of passion; a sapling pine
That grows on the edge of a Kansas bluff
And wars with wind when the weather is rough
Is like this Lasca, this love of mine.

"She would hunger that I might eat,
Would take the bitter and leave me the sweet;

But once, when I made her jealous for fun,
At something I'd whispered, or looked, or done,
One Sunday, in San Antonio,
To a glorious girl in the Alamo,
She drew from her garter a dear little dagger,
And—sting of a wasp!—it made me stagger!
An inch to the left, or an inch to the right,
And I shouldn't be maundering here tonight;
But she sobbed, and sobbing, so swiftly bound
Her torn reboso about the wound,
That I quite forgave her.
Scratches don't count
In Texas, down by the Rio Grande.

"Her eyes were brown—a deep, deep brown;
Her hair was darker than her eye;
And something in her smile and frown,
Curled crimson lip and instep high,
Showed that there ran in each blue vein,
Mixed with the milder Aztec strain,
The vigorous vintage of old Spain.
She was alive in every limb
With feeling to the finger tips;
And when the sun is like a fire,
And sky one shining, soft sapphire,
One does not drink in little sips.

"The air was heavy, and the night was hot,
I sat by her side, and forgot-forgot,
Forgot the herd that was taking their rest,
Forgot that the air was close opprest,
That the Texas norther comes sudden and soon,
In the dead of night or the blaze of noon;
That, once let the herd at its breath take fright,
Nothing on earth can stop its flight;
And woe to the rider, and woe to the steed,
Who falls in front of their mad stampede!

"Was that thunder? I grasped the cord
Of my swift mustang without a word.
I sprang to the saddle, and she clung behind.
Away? On a hot chase down the wind!
But never was a fox hunt half so hard,
And never was steed so little spared,
For we rode for our lives. You
Shall hear how we fared
In Texas, down by the Rio Grande.

"The mustang flew, and we urged him on;
There was one chance left, and you have but one;
Halt, jump to ground, and shoot your horse;
Crouch under his carcass and take your chance;
And, if the steers in their frantic course
Don't batter you both to pieces at once,
You may thank your star; if not good-bye
To the quickening kiss and the long-drawn sigh,
And the open air and the open sky,
In Texas, down by the Rio Grande.

"The cattle gained on us, just as I felt
For my old six-shooter behind my belt,
Down came the mustang, and down came we,
Clinging together—and what was the rest?
A body that spread itself on my breast,
Two arms that shielded my dizzy head,
Two lips that hard on my lips were pressed;
Then came thunder in my ears,
As over us surged the sea of steers,
Blows that beat blood into my eyes,
And when I could rise—Lasca was dead!

"I gouged out a grave a few feet deep,
And there in Earth's arms I laid her to sleep;
And there she is lying, and no one knows;
And the summer shines and the winter snows;
For many a day the flowers have spread

A pall of petals over her head;
And the little gray hawk hangs aloft in the air,
And the sly coyote trots here and there,
And the black snake glides and glitters and slides,
Into a rift in a cottonwood tree;
And the buzzard sails on, and comes and is gone,
Stately and still like a ship at sea,
And I wonder why I do not care
For the things that are like the things that were,
Does half my heart lie buried there
In Texas, down by the Rio Grande?"

John Robert's audience was silent as they thought about the old Texas folk poem. Then everyone gave him a big round of applause for his moving performance.

After that, everyone gathered around the piano with Lillie. Hardin took out his violin, and the family played and sang Christmas carols together long into the night.

It was a happy time for everyone on the farm!

Celebration

It's the miracle of life
When a tiny baby comes out.
So alive while facing life's strife,
She's perfect now, without a doubt.

Baby Edna changed the whole place.
People came from miles around.
They held her and treasured her face,
Loving her laughter and crying sound.

The Quest for Satisfaction

Something stirs within people that sets their personal goals higher each time they achieve the previous ones. As soon as mountain climbers successfully climb a high mountain, they desire to climb a higher one. They risk their lives just to know that they have achieved their personal best. If they live through that, they start planning more difficult climbs or challenges somewhere else.

When they first reach their goals, these individuals are elated and experience a great feeling of satisfaction. This feeling of success makes people feel so good that they desire to feel it again, and they can only achieve that by climbing a higher mountain and exceeding their personal best, using all that they have learned previously to do even more. This is why total and lasting satisfaction, that which drives us toward higher and higher goals in life, can never truly be achieved in a lasting way.

Hardin was achieving success on many fronts. He had found and married his true love, Lillie. They had a beautiful and precious baby, Edna. Hardin, J. Belt, Charles, and Clarence were running a prosperous farm. His parents lived close by, and they helped with the children and the family picnics on Sundays. Miss Emmy fit in well with the family and kept up the house so that all of the work didn't fall to Lillie.

Hardin's friend Rufus was a great partner in selecting and purchasing cattle and hogs to fatten. Frank Hall was his best friend and loved to visit with him when he was in town. When he was at home, Hardin enjoyed playing his violin while Lillie played the piano for the family. He often spent time reading interesting books in his study and enjoyed discussing them at the dinner table with Lillie and the children.

Hardin's favorite song was "Beautiful Dreamer," by Stephen Foster. He and Lillie often sat close to the warm fire in the fireplace while he played it on his violin and she accompanied him on the piano. They would sing together:

"Beautiful dreamer, wake unto me,
Starlight and dewdrops are waiting for thee."

Their sweet and loving words harmonized with the sounds of the piano and violin, and everyone who lived at Pleasant Valley Farm heard the music. It's melodic sound and sweet words brought peacefulness and bliss to Hardin's extended family as they settled down after dinner. It was their favorite song, and the beautiful music and words spoke to their mutual love and made Lillie and Harden feel even closer together on those winter evenings by the fire.

Hardin was at the top of his mountain now, and in time he would seek even more success and satisfaction as his ambitious life continued to grow and develop on Pleasant Valley Farm.

Happiness

Looking always higher,
Seeking love all around,
We quench our strong desire,
Happiness now is found.

But soon we reach a plateau,
And hover at that stage.
It's not enough for us, we know,
So again, we face our cage.

Growing Responsibilities

During the spring of 1890, Lillie found that she was with child again. Everything followed the pattern of her pregnancy with Edna, but something went wrong. Lillie's little baby was stillborn in the cold January of 1891. Hardin and Lillie were very sad, but they realized that many young babies did not survive.

Hardin became more active in local civic affairs as his influence in that area of Missouri grew. He met with the Farmers and Merchants board of directors monthly and was recognized as a more and more important asset to the bank. He made many friends and learned how businesses were run from the meetings.

St. Clair County was his community, and everyone respected Hardin for his hard work, excellent judgment, and honest values. He was very busy managing the farm, traveling to St. Louis, Kansas City, and Chicago on his stock marketing trips, and now he was also very active on the bank board and the Lowry City Council. It was clear to Hardin's family that he was an important part of their community. While he was often away from the farm, they understood that he needed his ongoing successes and achievements to be satisfied with his accomplishments in life.

In 1893, little baby Lillian was born. Lillie was happy, and they were both relieved that Lillian was a healthy, happy child. The family was growing.

In 1896, baby Harriet came. Now Lillie and Hardin had three children, and Lillie worked hard to keep the children healthy and happy.

Hardin noticed that Lillie was under a lot of strain even though Miss Emmy helped her as much as possible. John Robert and Mary Owen came over to help out with the kids when they could. Hardin also was concerned that John Robert was complaining more and more about feeling bad. He was out of breath easily and took a lot of naps in the afternoons.

Doc Stratton came and looked at both of them. He told Lillie that she needed to take better care of herself, and he prescribed a daily medicine for her to build up her strength. "She needs to rest more," Doc Stratton said.

When the Doc listened to John Robert's heart with his stethoscope, he had a worried look. "John Robert, you better take it easy too. Your heart is getting worn out," the doctor told him. Then he gave John Robert a prescription too.

Hardin was worried about them both and tried to stay home more to help out. He didn't ever want to lose Lillie or his dad. He still remembered the pain of loss that he had felt when Pearlie died, and it was almost too much to bear.

But you can never overcome a person's ultimate fate, and John Robert died quietly in his sleep one August evening in 1897. Ada, Claude, J. Belt, Hardin, and Lillie consoled Mary Owen as much as possible. John Robert had lived a good life for sixty-one years and had educated many Chalk Level and Pleasant Valley children during his lifetime.

There was a large funeral at the Baptist church, and he was buried in the church cemetery on the hill. Hardin's dad had been a wonderful father and family man. It was good that he had died on his beloved Fairy Glen Farm. Still, Hardin knew that his dad was gone from earth forever. His only hope was that he would rejoin his father in heaven someday. He prayed that the Lord would allow him to do so.

Mary Owen did not want to live alone on the Fairy Glen Farm. She moved to her daughter Ada's house and lived with her. It was a sad time in the Hammond family. They all needed time to adjust to the loss of John Robert.

Hardin spent even more evenings at home. He knew that his children needed him, and he was still concerned about Lillie. She just didn't look well, but Doc Stratton didn't know of anything else to do.

Children

Having children makes us satisfied,
But sometimes we are sad.
Lillie's little baby died,
Hearts broke in mother and dad.

Then came more babies small,
Lillie was weak, they say.
Happiness still encircled them all,
But she slipped a little each day.

Losing Lillie

Soon Lillie announced to Hardin that she was pregnant again. It was January 28, 1898, when little Mary Lilla (Marilee) Hammond was born. She was a lively little baby and brought new life into the house.

Two years later, Hardin Rodger Hammond was born. At last, Hardin had a son. He was ecstatic that he now had a boy to share the farm with.

The farm was now teeming with life. The Slagle boys still lived there, J. Belt was there when he wasn't staying in town, and Miss Emmy still cooked and cleaned for them. Hardin and Lillie had four girls and one boy to care for and all of the farm work to do. It was a busy time.

Hardin was becoming more and more worried about Lillie. She seemed to be doing too much, and she coughed a lot. She didn't look good, but still she pushed on, taking care of her growing family.

On July 28, 1900, the terrible tragedy that Hardin had been worried about happened without warning. Lillie was helping the children with their meal when suddenly her tired heart gave out. She fell to the kitchen floor and was dead in a minute. Her death was an awful blow to everyone at Pleasant Valley Farm. Hardin had lost his loving wife, and his five children had lost their mother. Hardin was shocked and heartbroken. His precious Lillie was gone. Lillie had only lived thirty-eight short years. Her death was the most tragic event that the family would ever endure.

Hardin was now a single father with five young children. It seemed that his God had let him down. His Lillie was gone, and nothing he had accomplished in his lifetime could replace her or her love. He cried and took long walks on the farm to try and make sense of his life. It wasn't fair. He had always believed that if you were good, good things would come to you. He felt guilty. What had he done wrong to deserve this loss? What had a good person such as Lillie done wrong to deserve losing her life?

It would take every bit of strength and determination Hardin had to pull himself and his family back together after Lillie's death. Right now, he just felt like giving up!

Loss

Sometimes we lose our true love,
With her precious heart and song.
Skyward flies the mourning dove,
Bearing the soul that's done no wrong.

Pain and hurt run through us all,
We question our belief.
Then children, farm, and parents call,
Only their love will ease our grief.

The Pain of Loss

A week after Lillie was buried in the Baptist church cemetery, Hardin found himself in shock. His body was without feeling, and he was in a state of confusion about his life. The funeral had been a large one; people had come from miles around to give his family support. They had wished to honor Lillie's beautiful spirit and meaningful life, which had been part of their community for eleven years.

The minister gave a brief history of Lillie's teaching career, her church activities, and her love of her children. The choir sang "Safe in the Arms of Jesus," "I Know Who Holds Tomorrow," and "Beyond the Sunset." The final song, at Hardin's request, was "Beautiful Dreamer."

Lillie was laid to rest in a grave close to John Robert's. The children cried as Hardin picked up some soil and anointed the casket with it, reciting "Ashes to ashes, dust to dust." Then she was gone.

Hardin looked at the obituary from the Osceola newspaper. It was brief and factual.

> Died from heart failure. July 28, 1900, Mrs. Lilla Hogan Hammond, aged thirty-eight years.
>
> Mrs. Hammond was born near Collinsville, Illinois, on March 4, 1862. She graduated from Belleville High School in her fifteenth year, and for several years previous to her marriage, she taught in the public schools. She united with the Old Bethel Baptist Church during the ministry of W. R. Andereck and was an earnest and efficient worker in Sunday school and church. On January 10, 1889, she married Mr. Hardin Hammond and moved to western Missouri. Six children were born of that union. Five children, the youngest a baby of nine months, survive the mother.

Without an instant of warning, Mrs. Hammond fell dead while ministering to her family. Thus she passed from an earthly world to a higher one and will surely be blessed by the love of God hereafter.

Hardin felt numb. Inside his body and mind, his feelings were suspended. It was as if his own existence had been taken from him without warning. He needed to hold on to his senses, and he was worried that he might go mad. Everything in his life was changed.

It was early Saturday morning. J. Belt had tied one on last night; drinking was his way of coping with the stress and tragedies in his life. The children were all sleeping except for the Slagle boys, who were automatically doing their livestock chores. Miss Emmy was quietly working in the kitchen, trying to keep the household routine together in this time of grief. She would be needed now more than ever, and she knew that there was no one else to take her place in the household.

The only thing that Hardin could think to do was to ride up to Old Baldy. He didn't want to be around anyone today. He was in too much shock to deal with the children or hear any talk about Lillie. He needed private time to adjust to his loss. He told Miss Emmy that he would be gone for the day but would be on the farm, then packed a few food items and headed for the barn.

Brownie was old now, but Hardin wanted to saddle him up to ride up on Old Baldy and be alone with his thoughts. He even threw his violin across the saddle in case he felt like playing. Hardin needed to do this today. He knew that he had to gather his thoughts and strength to keep from falling apart.

Brownie was his old friend, and he had taken Hardin on many adventures. The brown and white pony clip-clopped across Cooper's Bridge and up the trail slowly, sensing the sadness and loneliness of his rider. When they arrived at the top, Hardin dismounted and sat on the old, weathered log. Brownie grazed on the leaves and grass that grew on the hill in late July.

Hardin just sat and felt the peacefulness of the hill. The sun was glowing stronger as it rose past the far hills. Hardin let his mind go deep inside his soul, searching for answers that would not come. The tears that rolled down his cheeks felt somehow blessed, as if Lillie were there, soothing him gently. Brownie stayed close by, then came over and nuzzled Hardin's neck. The old horse was still there for Hardin.

The log, Brownie, and the peaceful hill gave Hardin solace. They gave him time to allow his senses to recover as much as possible. His deep sense of values gave him the inner strength to help overcome the pain he was feeling. Hardin just sat still. He was sad and lonely. His mind was filled with the sweet memories of Lillie as the day passed into late afternoon.

As the sun began its downward drift toward the western horizon, Hardin realized that his life had changed and that he needed to direct it the way that would be "right" for himself and his family.

Hardin mounted Brownie and rode down the hill slowly and with resolution. He would spend as much time that he could with the children. They needed him more than ever, and he needed them just as badly. Then he would throw himself into his work. Work was the one constant in his life that gave him satisfaction.

The next morning, Hardin stayed and had breakfast with his children, then rode off to meet Rufus for the day's stock-buying trip to the town of Deepwater.

Tonight there would be no sweet Lillie to greet him when he got home. He would play his violin for the children after dinner. Perhaps he would read to them later. He knew how important it was to be brave and try to maintain a normal life for everyone at Pleasant Valley Farm as much as possible.

It would be a long time until Hardin's loss became lingering, bittersweet memories. In time, he would realize that he would survive this terrible tragedy. Thank goodness he had his children and his family's love to sustain his ragged soul during this difficult time in his life.

Process

Thinking deep inside our pain,
We wonder why and how.
Unsure that we are sane,
Nothing matters to us now.

Then slowly, we realize our sin
Now that she is gone.
Do our best, try hard again,
Her voice speaks to us, "Go on! Go on!"

Minnie Etta Slavens

Across the Osage River from Pleasant Valley Farm, Minnie Slavens knelt on the cold, wooden floor of the Kennerly Chapel for a long time, praying for her family and loved ones. Her legs were numb in the chill during that church service in January 1900. At thirty-two years of age, Minnie had seen few romances during her lifetime. Her strong will and intelligence often seemed to close the door to qualified suitors. Now she prayed for happiness in life and that she would someday have small children and a man to help her raise a family of her own.

Rising on her feet, Minnie walked to the front of the church to take her place at the organ and lead the church choir. They sang "Bringing in the Sheaves" and "What a Friend We Have in Jesus." Minnie provided leadership to the small choir as they soothed the souls of the congregation with their music. The sweet music warmed the hearts of the choir and the congregation, which was made up of so many of Minnie's family and friends. The songs gave them hope for the future.

The Kennerly Chapel, a Methodist church, provided Minnie with many friends and the personal satisfaction of giving to her community. The chapel itself was named after a Confederate soldier, William Kennerly, who was famous in Missouri for his stubbornness at the end of the war. He was one of three Confederates who did not surrender when the papers were being signed at the Appomattox courthouse; they just turned their horses and rode away to go back home to their families. The Kennerly Chapel reminded everyone of the strong conviction and pride of William Kennerly. The church gave Minnie a reason for being, and its history was a constant reminder of the importance of standing up for one's principles and values.

The social time after church services was fun for Minnie. Her father, Henry Balis Slavens, attended the stone church as well as many of her fifteen brothers and sisters, many with spouses and children. It was both a weekly family event and a time for Minnie to act as a central figure in the church community. She was the event organizer and music director for the church.

Minnie was a proud woman with a beautiful and intelligent face. She was always well dressed, and she was highly respected in the community. Her expression was generally somewhat formal, giving others the impression that she was rather businesslike. Still, there was a loving and caring woman inside. She demonstrated her generosity and helpfulness to her family each day. Her strength and decisive ways were an important part of the Slavens household. Her strong personality had not yet allowed for romance in her life, but she hoped that someday the right man would come along. For the moment, Minnie had a good life and was making the best of it.

That evening, Minnie knelt by her bedside for her evening prayers. Then she lay awake in bed for a long time, wondering about her future. When her brothers and sisters were all married and gone, maybe she would travel to California and start a new life. When the time was right, that would a good thing for her to do. With that hopeful thought, Minnie closed her eyes and drifted off to sleep.

Trying

The church was simple and cold,
Minnie knelt on the floor there.
Her bearing was smart and bold,
As God held her in his care.

She wasn't the local beauty;
Many suitors had passed her by.
But fate and fortune rewarded duty
When handsome Hardin came riding by.

Coping with Life Alone

It is said that whatever doesn't kill you makes you stronger. Hardin's depression over the loss of Lillie stayed with him for a very long time. Friends and relatives made special attempts to help him forget his loss and accept his new life, but cheering him up was impossible; the memories of his happy life with Lillie constantly ran through his mind. It was impossible for him to visualize any other happiness similar to what he had experienced with Lillie. His future without her presence in his life seemed so empty. Hardin concentrated on raising his children and working on building up the farm.

Hardin was now a handsome widower with a prosperous farm. He also had the five children, the Slagle boys, J. Belt, and Miss Emmy living on the farm. There were many single women in the area who wished to become better acquainted with Hardin, but he had no interest in them. He just wasn't ready for a new relationship.

Hardin thought about his children and how he wanted to raise them. He realized that when a parent sets an example for his children, the children honored and emulated that example more than any words they may hear. "Actions speak louder than words," he thought. With this in mind, Hardin renewed his resolve to be honest and hard working, dress appropriately, communicate with his children as often as possible, and play with them when he could.

Before Lillie had died, Hardin would often come home late or leave the farm on business trips. Now Hardin realized that he was all the children had, and he rearranged his priorities so that he could be with them more. He even planned special events with each child, often taking them on horseback rides or coming home to have lunch with the small ones. The children were his life, and Hardin loved his closeness with them.

His weeks became structured for their benefit. In the evenings, he would read their favorite stories to them. Then, before bedtime, he would play two or three of their favorite tunes on his violin. Hardin's sorrow slowly changed into the realization that his family needed him more than ever. His feelings about himself and his life took on new meaning as he struggled with his responsibilities during the years after Lillie's untimely death.

Hardin's life became more rewarding over time, but he still felt an emptiness inside that he could not fill. By 1902, Little Hardin Rodgers was two years old, Mary Lilla was four, Harriet was six, Lillian was nine, and Edna was thirteen. Charlie and Clarence were twenty-three and twenty-five. J. Belt helped out on the farm when he was there and not off drinking. Faithful Miss Emmy kept everything organized and put good food on the table. It was still a busy household.

The Pleasant Valley School hired a new teacher, Ruth Brown. She needed a place to live, and Hardin added her to the list of occupants on the farm. She would be good to have around in the evenings, and perhaps she could help with his children's education.

In the third year after Lillie had passed away, Hardin put all his daytime energy into building the Pleasant Valley Stock Farm. He and Rufus still visited families in neighboring towns, buying up livestock to be fattened for the market. Hardin also still attended the board of directors meetings held monthly in Osceola for the Farmers and Merchants Bank, and every two weeks, he attended the evening meeting of the Lowry City Council. Sundays were reserved for church and family get-togethers.

Hardin found the women he met pleasant and attractive, but in June of 1904, he became interested in a special woman in a neighboring town. There seemed to be a spark between them. Hardin began thinking about the possibilities of having a relationship again. He was now forty-three years old.

"Could it be so?" he thought to himself.

Adjusting

Hardin gave his loving all
To children and parents too.
His dedication was his call,
That they needed him was true.

Forsaking all other women,
When his true love, Lillie, died,
Hardin's heart just couldn't win,
As all alone at night he cried.

Hardin's Renewal

Hardin and Rufus were on a stock-buying trip at the Slavens' home near El Dorado Springs on June 1, 1904. El Dorado Springs was a town about fifteen miles from the Pleasant Valley Farm across the swift and deep Osage River. As was customary, Minnie's father, Henry Balis Slavens, invited them to stay for lunch.

Hardin saw at once that Minnie, who was sitting across the table from him, was intelligent and attractive. She led the conversation and was obviously interested in him and his family. After lunch, Minnie played several songs on the piano. Hardin wistfully remembered the wonderful evenings that he had enjoyed with Lillie. He became excited about the possibilities that Minnie offered as a companion.

Hardin and Minnie took a private walk around the farm and learned more and more about their common interests and values. Hardin confessed many things about his lonely existence, working and raising the children. Minnie felt compassion for this handsome and lonely widower. She wondered how it would be to live with him and take care of his household. She liked Hardin very much and hoped to see him again.

When Hardin and Rufus finally had to leave, Hardin promised Minnie that he would write to her and visit with her again when possible. Hardin was a man of his word and always followed through on the promises he made.

As Rufus and Hardin rode through the evening and crossed the bridge at Osceola, Hardin felt an excitement and joy that he had not felt for more than four years. Minnie was attractive and interesting, yet challenging with her strong personality. He thought that she would be a good partner with whom he could spend the rest of his life. He would write to her tonight and plan another visit to the Slavens' farm as soon as possible. It would be fun to go on a picnic with her, bring his violin, and enjoy music in her pleasant company.

Hardin was thrilled about the opportunity for a new life with Minnie. He hoped that Minnie was feeling the same way.

Together

No one knows what fate and love will bring
When both have given up.
Then surprise makes our heart sing
As chance moves in and fills its cup.

Invisible rays cross the blue,
Then spark the mating game.
It flickers, now strong and true,
Soon nothing ever will be the same.

A Difficult Romance

The next morning, Hardin couldn't wait to write his letter and get it into the day's mail. As soon as he had eaten his breakfast, he retired to his study and wrote to Minnie.

Dear Minnie,

I enjoyed so very much the opportunity to meet you yesterday and enjoy your company. It has been a long time since I have walked and talked with someone who has made me feel so comfortable. I also enjoyed the excellent music that you played on your piano. It brought back fond memories of happier times.

Minnie, I feel that you are a special person. I wish to know much more about you. I was wondering if I came to your home on the Sunday after next, might we enjoy a country picnic together? I will bring the buggy and a picnic basket. I would also like to play my violin for you. I will bring it along too.

I am hopeful that you are available on that day and that your answer will be yes. Please write me as soon as you can.

Awaiting your reply,
Hardin

It was seven long days before Hardin received Minnie's reply.

Dear Hardin,

I was thrilled to receive your letter following your visit last week. My, you don't waste any time, do you?

A Sunday afternoon picnic with you sounds like so much fun. I am anxious to hear you play the violin.

Church gets out at 11:30. I play the organ for the choir, so I will be needed until then. Please don't worry about the food. As you are traveling all this way, allow me to make up the basket. I hope that you like fried chicken, potato salad, and other fixings.

Unless I hear otherwise, I shall be looking forward to seeing you on the Sunday after next.

Affectionately yours,
Minnie

Hardin read the letter several times, looking for hidden meaning. Her parting words, "affectionately yours," gave him confidence in their budding relationship and promised to him more than just friendship.

Each evening as Hardin lay in bed before sleeping, he pictured the upcoming picnic with Minnie in his mind. He would ask her for a suggestion of a good picnic spot, but if she didn't have one, he would seek a hill or bluff with a nice view for them to picnic on. Hardin knew that talking with Minnie would be stimulating, but he also needed holding, touching, kissing, and whatever followed. Hardin needed Minnie to love him and to let him know that she was attracted to him in a sensual way. If she could love him, nothing would stop him from pursuing their relationship further.

It was time for Hardin to start looking ahead to his future.

Hope

Your heart beats so much faster,
Beautiful images float in your mind.
Just when your life saw disaster,
Your soul finds love in kind.

Now take action, step into the fray,
She may need you too.
Without fail, ask her today,
And speak of your love so true.

A Picnic with Minnie

Hardin pulled up at the Slavens' farmhouse in his buggy promptly at noon. He was clean and dressed in his Sunday attire for his picnic with Minnie. He was so looking forward to their outing and hoped that she was as he remembered her—pretty and interesting with a touch of confidence that challenged his senses. He would not be disappointed.

Minnie came to the door in an attractive blue skirt and a red blouse that accentuated her ample breasts and pretty shape. Hardin found her sexy and animated as they walked to the buggy. He held her hand as she stepped up on her side and sat down. Hardin entered on the other side and took the reins. They headed down the road, and Minnie told Hardin which way to go.

Minnie chatted about her morning at church. She noted that her minister had made a fine sermon about vices that people fall into, such as drinking alcohol. She was a member of the local Women's Christians Temperance Union and had received a silver medal for a speech she had given on the subject of temperance last year.

Hardin told her that he never touched alcohol as he felt that it impaired one's senses. He was sorry to admit that his older brother, J. Belt, was a drinker despite Hardin's admonishments. J. Belt came home under the influence far too often.

Hardin told Minnie about his life's motto, "Endeavor to do right." He talked about his philosophy of setting a good example for others, especially your children. Then Hardin told Minnie about his large household: how he had taken in the Slagle boys; how John Robert had died; and about the schoolteacher, Ruth Brown, the housekeeper Miss Emmy, and J. Belt. He told Minnie about how J. Belt helped out with the farming when he was needed. Hardin was trying to do right by helping all of these people while raising five children of his own.

"Are you happy, Hardin?" Minnie gently asked.

Hardin didn't know how to answer that question. After a long silence, he answered. His eyes were moist as he confessed that he just was trying to do the right thing for everyone. His God had let him down so many times: when his sister Pearlie had died, when his father had died, and when Lillie had passed away so suddenly. He wasn't sure what happiness was anymore. He just worked hard and led what he thought was a righteous life, hoping that the payoff would be happiness and eternal life. So far, Hardin felt that his life had been filled with mixed blessings, but he would continue to live by his principles until he died.

Minnie's hand slid slowly across the buggy seat, and she softly wrapped her smooth fingers around Hardin's. The comfort that Hardin found in her touch filled him and covered his worn soul. Hardin held her hand in his, and warmth spread over his body. She was there for him with understanding and compassion, and that brought him happiness that he hadn't felt for years. Hardin thanked God for this moment and wished he could live it forever. Minnie was bringing love back into Hardin's life.

She chose a high bluff overlooking the valley for their picnic. Hardin made a small fire, and they spread out the blanket that Hardin had brought to sit upon. Minnie's picnic basket was loaded with fried chicken, potato salad, bread, and a blackberry pie that she had made. They set the food out on the blanket and were preparing to eat when Hardin brought a brown paper sack out of the buggy. Hardin handed Minnie the sack and sat down beside her.

"I brought you a present that I thought you might like," he said.

Minnie reached into the sack and brought out a small, rectangular package wrapped in gold paper. She held the small package close to her bosom for a minute, treasuring the thought that Hardin had brought her a special gift.

Minnie's hands were shaking slightly as she removed the gold paper. Inside, she discovered a beautiful, leather-bound book. It was a compilation of the poems that the famous Englishman George Gordon Lord Byron had written before his early death at age thirty-six. Lord Byron's poetry, known for its beauty and eloquence, was revered throughout the world for its depth and perception.

Inside the cover, Hardin had written on the first page.

To Minnie, with love,
Hardin R. Hammond
St. Clair Co.
Osceola, MO

"Oh, Hardin, I couldn't be more pleased. Thank you so much for this beautiful book of Lord Byron's poems. I shall treasure it throughout my lifetime," Minnie said emotionally as she admired the leather cover and glanced at the pages inside.

"Minnie, I have a very special poem that I would like to share with you. It reminds me of you and is very special to me. If you don't mind, I will read it to you now."

"Please do, Hardin. I would love to hear you read his poetry. It can only heighten my gratitude to you for this very special gift."

Hardin turned to the page that held a printed bookmark. Looking at Minnie, Hardin began to read, slowly and with feeling.

"She walks in beauty, like the night
Of cloudless climes and starry skies."

His soft voice spoke the timeless words of beauty and love as he read the poem to Minnie. His passion for her was clear, and his reading of the carefully chosen poetry expressed so well the love that Hardin felt for her on that quiet summer evening.

When Hardin finished reading the poem to her, Minnie sat silent and still, looking far out into the valley. She felt her heart beating with joy. There was so much promise of happiness and love with this man.

Finally, Minnie turned to Hardin. Taking both of his hands in hers, she spoke with the hint of soft emotion in her voice.

"Thank you, Hardin, for your wonderful gift. Your reading of Lord Byron's poem here upon this hill is so very special. I will never forget your thoughtfulness and words. At this moment, I feel your love. You have captured my heart!"

They kissed and held each other for a long time. Finally, they ate and talked about their lives with animation throughout the afternoon. It was clear to both of them that they were in love. Minnie laid her head on Hardin's shoulder as he lay on his back, looking at the clouds.

As the sun began to set, Hardin's kisses met her willing ones in the warm and wonderful passion of love and desire. It grew dark, and they wanted to stay the night together right there, kissing and making love, but they both knew that they had too many responsibilities at home and had to go.

Hardin drove the buggy slowly back down to the farm. Minnie was cuddled against him with her head on his shoulder, and it felt so good that he wanted to prolong the trip as long as possible. When they said good-bye at her door, Hardin vowed to write or see her as soon as possible. He could not know that the Osage would flood, making his next visit impossible until the river subsided.

Hardin drove slowly home, wondering if Minnie would marry him and help him take on the responsibilities of his large family. If only she would, he would be happier than he had been in a long, long time.

Searching

He drank her beauty,
Saw style and grace.
Her life filled with duty,
Compassion showed on her face.

"Are you happy?" she queried.
Hardin's hand brushed his hair,
He seemed so worried,
She saw the tears there.

A Summer of Floods

Hardin wrote to Minnie the next day.

My dearest Minnie,

My time with you yesterday meant more to me than I could have ever imagined. You are the woman who has been missing from my life and my happiness. I am hoping to spend as much time with you as possible. I am very hopeful that you will be able to see me soon. I shall be glad to come to El Dorado Springs when you are available. Perhaps the Saturday after next would be a good day? I will be anxiously waiting for your reply.

All my love,
Hardin

A week later Hardin, received Minnie's reply.

Dear Hardin,

I have never felt as comfortable with a man as I do with you. You are handsome and commanding, and any woman would be proud to be with you. I will be awaiting your visit when you come to El Dorado Springs in two weeks. I very much look forward to the time when we will be together again.

Love,
Minnie

J. Belt noticed that Hardin was smiling and laughing a lot more lately. He suspected that it had to do with that Slavens woman Hardin had been seeing in El Dorado Springs. It made J. Belt happy to see Hardin smile again. Hardin had been sad and unhappy since he had lost Lillie. J. Belt loved his younger brother and would do anything for him. He hoped that Hardin's relationship would last and continue to bloom.

A few days before Hardin was to set out to see Minnie, the skies darkened and opened up, and it rained for days. The road to the bridge at Osceola was the only way to cross the Osage River, and the road leading up to the bridge was very low. The river flooded over the road in only three days, so now there was no way for him to go see Minnie.

Hardin was upset and unhappy. He quickly wrote Minnie of his frustration and how he would have to put off his visit for at least two weeks. He told her that he would come as soon as the road was open.

An old friend of Hardin's, Tom Dark, had found a way to cross the flooded waters of the Osage River. Tom had a sturdy rowboat that he used to reach Osceola. Then he could saddle up his stabled horse and ride to towns on the eastern side of the river.

Hardin called upon his friendship with Tom Dark. Tom agreed to make periodic trips to El Dorado Springs. Tom delivered Hardin's letters to Minnie and brought her letters back to Hardin. The post office wasn't delivering mail across the flooded Osage River at that time, but Tom was glad to help Hardin to repay him for helping him out when he had needed work to feed his family.

After ten days, Minnie's reply came. Hardin was relieved that she understood about the flood. She would be glad to see him whenever he could come.

Finally, in early July, Hardin and Minnie finally saw each other again. They went to the same spot for another picnic. Hardin had made up his mind. He proposed to Minnie right there on the bluff and brought a small, velvet-covered, black box out of his coat pocket.

As Hardin opened the ring box, Minnie's eyes begin to tear. She took the expensive diamond engagement ring out of the box. She held the ring in her closed hand and clasped it tightly to her heart. Then, looking deep into Hardin's eyes, she put her hands in his. Hardin was thrilled by her warm look and touch. He knew then that she loved him deeply and that her answer would be yes.

"Yes," she said softly. "Hardin, I will marry you. You have made me very happy. I pledge to you that I will be a good and loving wife."

Hardin gently slipped the engagement ring onto her finger. They kissed and embraced each other tightly, seeking the warmth and love for which they both hungered so much. They lay on the blanket far into the night, hugging and kissing and talking about their future together.

They both wanted to be married as soon as possible. The floods couldn't separate them once they were together. She would come and live on Pleasant Valley Farm. He was sure that she would like everyone there. They could play music together and sing in the evenings.

Minnie and Hardin couldn't wait to tell her parents and all of their other relatives. They drove the buggy down the hill and announced to the Slavens family that they were to be married. They planned to have their wedding in Kansas City, Missouri, on August 29, 1904. It would be a beautiful wedding, but the honeymoon would be somewhat unusual.

Barriers

Rivers wide and mountains high
Seem to us a sin.
But love's trick makes us sigh
As time grows feelings from within.

Through the weather we find ways
To cross the abyss between,
Love sends thoughts through the haze,
As romance grows strong and clean.

A New Life

Minnie stayed with her sister, Nellie High, in Kansas City for the week before the wedding. They went shopping during that time and bought her trousseau. Her wedding dress was a light gray silk with tiny black dots. She also purchased white silk hose as an intriguing part of her sleeping attire.

J. Belt was Hardin's best man, and Nellie was the maid of honor. Both families were in attendance, and Minnie and Hardin exchanged marriage vows in the beautiful Baptist church in downtown Kansas City. The wedding ceremony was followed by a reception with food and drink in the same building.

For their honeymoon, they attended the World's Fair in St. Louis. Strange as it may seem, they were accompanied on their honeymoon trip by Minnie's sister Nellie, her husband Charles, and Hardin's oldest daughter Edna, who was fifteen. They were all happy with the arrangement and enjoyed the attractions at the 1904 World's Fair very much. After their honeymoon, Hardin and Minnie went directly to Pleasant Valley Farm. The farm would now be Minnie's new home.

When they arrived at the farm, Minnie met the rest of Hardin's household. Hardin proudly introduced her to the other four children; she met Lillian, Harriet, Mary Lilla, and Hardin R. Hardin R. was the youngest at just four years old. She also met Clarence and Charlie Slagle, and Miss Emmy. Minnie was informed that they boarded the Pleasant Valley schoolteacher, Ruth Brown, during the winter months. Pleasant Valley Farm seemed more like a small town than a farm to her, but she took the challenges in stride and worked on being a friend to each and every occupant.

It was a good thing that Minnie was a strong woman and made friends easily. She soon took charge of the formidable household, and once again Hardin had a home instead of merely a house to come home to.

Hardin was now forty-three years old, and Minnie was thirty-two. They were embarking on a new life together. It promised to be a great adventure. Hardin was happy. He now had someone to share his dreams with again. Minnie was the woman he wanted to come home to at the end of every day.

Hardin and Minnie Hammond

Pleasant Valley Farm was a happy household once again with many personalities working together for growth and survival in the Missouri backcountry. Minnie found that the children needed her. She took her responsibilities seriously and drew the young ones close to her as she watched over them. Minnie wanted to be a good wife to Hardin and a good mother to the children.

Grandparents

Grandpa Hardin and Minnie married,
Kansas City was the place in 1904.
Aunt Nellie helped, Minnie was harried,
Preparing the wedding was quite a chore.

*Honeymoon at the World's Fair,
Then off to Pleasant Valley Farm.
The house was full of people there,
Minnie fit in with grace and charm.*

Renewal and Discovery

——————— ❧ ———————

Hardin had always thought that being a good businessman and developing Pleasant Valley Stock Farm would automatically lead to his happiness. The four years he'd spent as a single father had caused him to look at his life critically as he sought personal happiness again.

He found that hard work and material success brought him some satisfaction, but the inner Hardin had experienced strong feelings of self-doubt and worthlessness. He was very busy all of the time, but his many activities only shielded him from the sadness inside. He hoped that others would not see through his efforts to appear normal and cheerful. Unfortunately, inner sadness always shows itself to other people through one's appearance, mannerisms, and personality. It cannot be hidden from others for very long.

Hardin's values had changed since Lillie had died. He now realized that each individual under his care was special and often emotionally fragile. He had learned to spend more time at home with his family and to enjoy them as they grew up. As he grew closer to his family, he found that he had the strength and intelligence to deal with the daily hardships of raising children.

Hardin remembered that every obstacle in life had a benefit or solution if one's mind is open to looking for it. He learned that if he was worried about something when he went to bed at night, such as problems with the children or with money, he could think about other things, relax his mind, and go to sleep.

One of his favorite things to imagine as he drifted off to sleep was sitting on a blanket under his favorite tree on Old Baldy. In his imagination, he was alone, looking out over the farm and enjoying the squirrels and birds that came close to him as he sat motionless, thinking about his life.

He also could bring to mind a picture of a large, endless wheat field, the brown tops blowing in unison in the breeze, gently swaying in rhythm. When he thought about the gentle wheat field, he was always soothed to sleep.

The Hardin that Minnie married was a much stronger and more independent man than the one he had been four years earlier. He had learned to cope with the difficulties in his life and to overcome them. Minnie found in Hardin a man whom she could trust and who was not moody or irritable. Her growing happiness and satisfaction demonstrated to her that he was the right choice for her. She wanted him to be the father of her children. They would be a team, raising their children together through the years.

Minnie was an accomplished pianist, so she and Hardin loved to play together in the evenings for the family. Hardin would play his violin along with her piano tunes. Often, the whole family would sing along to the music. Hardin found that he could buy a fine, black, mahogany grand piano from Germany and have it imported. He contacted the dealer and had one shipped to the farm for Minnie. When it was delivered, Minnie's eyes shone with delight. What a special gift Hardin had given her! These were the happiest of times.

It wasn't long before Minnie was pregnant. They both eagerly waited for the day that their first child would be born. On June 28, 1905, Zelma Owen Hammond was born. She was a cute baby and very active. Both Hardin and Minnie adored her, as did the other children. Many eager and loving hands held little Zelma.

After a year or so, Hardin and Minnie were elated when Minnie became pregnant again. Little Doris Arline Hammond was born on Pleasant Valley Farm on January 30, 1907. The family was growing, and Minnie kept very busy taking care of the children as Hardin turned his attention to the farm.

Hardin realized that he would have to work very hard in the coming years to support his growing family. He turned his attention to business, traveling to St. Louis, Kansas City, and Chicago to market his cattle and hogs. He was feeding around one hundred cattle and two hundred hogs on the farm. He also managed the crops, horses, and other animals that were an important part of his operation.

Hardin was building a prosperous farm for himself and his family. He was as happy as he had ever been, but in July of 1907, a terrible tragedy changed the future of the Pleasant Valley Stock Farm. It was an unexpected, undeserved, and unbelievable disaster that also changed the history of Hardin Hammond's family forever.

Rebirth

Happiness and love return,
Life's miracle was there.

Minnie's first child, Hardin would learn,
Had his blue eyes and brown hair.

The second baby was my mother Arline,
Her determination showed clearly through.
With special energy she changed the scene,
Someday she would teach with conviction true.

Life's Mystery

It is difficult to understand why good people are often taken from this earth at a time when they are at the zenith of their productivity and goodness. One's life can be taken away at any time, so we must always remember that our presence on this earth is temporary. No matter how long we live, we will die in the end.

Many make it to a very old age if they are lucky, live a healthy lifestyle, and inherit longevity genes. Others die when they are infants, young adults, middle aged, or at the start of old age. We never really know just how long we will live. We must seek to make the best of our lives each day. If we make a difference in our own personal happiness or someone else's, we can know that our lives on this earth were worthwhile.

Life's satisfaction comes as we pass through it, making the best of each day and building our heritage for others to follow. In the end, we can only leave the spirit of how we lived to our ancestors. Our legacy of values and accomplishments sets the standard for future generations.

And so it was with Hardin, my good and industrious grandfather, who became ill one day in late July. It was one of the hottest days of the year. Hardin rode a few miles west on the farm to load some cattle. He was going to ship a carload of cattle and a carload of hogs to Kansas City on that day. The morning was filled with hard labor as Hardin and the Slagle boys pushed and prodded the animals into the wagons to be taken to the railroad in Osceola. The sweat poured off of Hardin as he loaded the animals under the hot Missouri sun.

At noon, the men took a break for lunch. Hardin wasn't feeling very well, but he sat down at the table to eat. He noticed a pain in his stomach that grew into violent cramping. Hardin decided that it would be best for him to lie down after lunch. Shipping the animals would have to wait another day.

Minnie was very concerned; Hardin's condition was getting worse by the hour. She summoned Dr. Stratton, who arrived early that evening. After examining Hardin, Dr. Stratton thought that Hardin had either locked bowels or appendicitis, but he wasn't sure which. Either condition was serious. He gave Hardin some medicine and said he would check on him the next day.

Minnie summoned two other physicians late on the second day of Hardin's illness, and they stayed at the farm in a concentrated effort to alleviate his suffering. He was in a precarious condition, and his physicians determined that his chances of recovering were becoming slimmer.

Minnie brought cold compresses to alleviate Hardin's fever and stayed by his side to comfort him. His condition seemed to be improving steadily after a few days, but he suffered a serious relapse late one afternoon, and the physician was summoned again. J. Belt paced the floor of the bedroom while Minnie sat beside Hardin, deeply worried. If only they could think of a way to make him well, but it was too late!

Hardin motioned to J. Belt to come over by the bed. Looking and pointing upward, Hardin said weakly to J. Belt, "It looks bright up yonder." Then Hardin's eyes closed forever as the life that had shone so brightly left his body.

On July 29, 1907, Hardin Hammond, the grandfather I never met who fathered my mother, watched over many other children, and was respected by his community, passed away while surrounded by his loving family. He was only forty-six years old. My mother was six months old at the time of his death.

Hardin's obituary read as follows:

HARDIN R. HAMMOND

Hardin R. Hammond, whose critical illness was noted last week, died at the family residence in Chalk Level Township last Monday afternoon at 6:30 PM. His remains were laid to rest in the Concord Cemetery on Tuesday afternoon.

Mr. Hammond was born in Cass County on April 7, 1861, to the late John R. Hammond and Mary Owen Hammond. He moved to St. Clair County with his parents in 1866, where he has since resided.

Elder D. B. Warren furnishes the following sketch of the deceased.

He was married to Miss Lillie Hogan at Collinsville, IL, on January 10, 1889. To this union were born six children, five of them surviving him. His wife died on July 28, 1900.

He was married again to Miss Minnie E. Slavens on August 29, 1904. To this union two children were born, and both are living. Of his close relatives, there remain to mourn his departure his wife and seven children, his mother, two brothers, and one sister.

Shortly before his first marriage, he confessed his faith in Christ and was baptized by Elder J. H. Jones, now of Bolivar, MO. He often talked to the writer about the Christian religion and expressed a desire to live closer to God. Soon after he became seriously ill, he expressed doubts about his recovery to his brother, J. Belt Hammond, and pointing upward, said, "It looks bright up yonder."

May the good Lord bless and comfort the bereaved and enable us to answer the summons when the death angel calls.

Mr. Hammond was an enterprising farmer and stock dealer, and at the time of his death he was feeding about one hundred head of cattle and two hundred hogs. The day that he was taken ill, he shipped off one fattened carload of each, and it is probable that this hard labor in the boiling sun was the primary cause of his illness. He was a member of the Lowry City Chamber of Commerce and a member of the board of directors of the Farmers and Merchants Bank of Osceola. Mr. Hammond will be sorely missed in our community.

Heartbroken

Everything changed so fast
At Pleasant Valley Farm that day.
Tragedy struck! Before it was past,
They carried poor Hardin away.

Shocked with loss, Minnie cried.
Hardin's precious life was through.
The love of her life had suddenly died,
Now what would she do?

Good-bye, Beloved Hardin

The funeral, which was held at the Baptist church and the Concord Cemetery, was clothed in deep sorrow. Everyone felt the loss of Hardin's bright presence in the community.

Minnie wore a black dress and a wide-brimmed, black hat with a veil over her face. J. Belt stood on one side of her, and Nellie High was on the other as they helped her down the aisle of the church and seated her in front. She could barely walk, and her legs shook visibly. The large crowd in the church looked on sadly and with deep sympathy.

In the attractive, mahogany coffin lined with lavender silk lay Hardin, whose handsome features looked as if he were still living and was just resting. He was dressed in his full Sunday attire and his black, vested suit. His white tie and shirt and the neatly folded white handkerchief showing in his chest pocket gave him dignity in his attractive casket.

The family was seated in the first two rows on the left side of the aisle. The older girls watched after Zelma, Arline, and little Hardin and helped out where they could.

The onlookers, many of whom were crying and dabbing their moist eyes, knew that this was a tragedy of huge proportions for the Hammond family. What would become of them without Hardin? What would Minnie do with this huge responsibility?

Silently, many pledged their support to help Minnie and the family get through the coming weeks and months. They knew that she would need all of the help she could get.

The minister opened with a few passages from the Bible, and everyone prayed with him for the resurrection of Hardin's soul in heaven. Then the minister talked about how nobody knew why Hardin's good life had been taken, but God, in his master plan, had chosen for Hardin to pass to a higher life at that time.

At Minnie's request, two of Hardin's favorite songs were sung, accompanied by the church piano. There was crying and sobbing throughout the church as the congregation first sang "Amazing Grace" and then followed with his very favorite song, "Beautiful Dreamer." The singing rang out through the church and into the hills that he had loved so much. The song embodied Hardin's love for his family, the people in his community, and especially his love for Minnie that had brought him so much happiness in his last few years on earth.

Then Hardin's eighteen-year-old daughter Edna, very attractive and poised in her black dress, walked up to the podium. She said, "I have written a poem in honor of my father and the message that he left with me."

"'Hardin'

"Yesterday I walked with bleary eyes
Down the lane as my heart cries,
To the bridge on Cooper's Creek,
My father's message I wished to seek.

"The waters told me nothing new,
Nothing, no message for me or you.
I thought his spirit must be here,
Father that I love so dear.

"Then my eyes went to the hill,
Where father's soul might linger still.
Far off, something climbed Old Baldy's trail,
I knew the form, let out a wail.

"It was Father walking to the top,
When he reached it, he didn't stop.
Into the sky he plodded on
Toward the clouds; he was almost gone.

"To soothe his soul and peace of mind,
Faithful Brownie followed right behind.
Finally I saw Big Black
Tagging along in Hardin's track.

"Heaven waits for them above,
A glorious tribute to Father's love.
Where we will meet with them someday
To find eternal life along the way.

"A wave, a smile, he disappeared;
It was the moment that I feared.
I sought the message, and it came to me:
Father, with my soul, I love thee."

Beautiful Edna returned to her place as everyone considered her thought-provoking poem about her father. Her message to them was that he would be okay now that he was in heaven. They would join him someday.

Finally, before placing Hardin in his final resting place, everyone repeated the twenty-third psalm in unison.

"The Lord is my shepherd; I shall not want.
He makes me lie down in green pastures.
He leads me beside quiet waters.
He restores my soul.
He guides me in paths of righteousness for his name's sake.
Even though I walk through the valley of the shadow of death,
I will fear no evil,
For you are with me.
Your rod and your staff, they comfort me.
You prepare a table in the midst of my enemies.
You anoint my head with oil.
My cup overflows.
Surely goodness and love will follow me all the days of my life.
And I will dwell in the house of the Lord forever.

Amen."

Everyone passed by Hardin's casket for one final look at the man who had done so much in his short life on earth. The family passed by last, and Minnie looked at him with tears and a broken heart. She and her family were led to their seats of honor next to the open grave. The now closed casket was lowered as the minister softly recited passages from the Bible. Minnie sprinkled some dust upon the casket and requested to stay alone by the grave as the well-wishers left to go to the farm for a reception.

J. Belt and Nellie waited in the buggy as Minnie sat in the cemetery. She did not want to leave Hardin's side because she knew that it would be her last time with him. After more than an hour, she signaled them to come help her to the buggy. They drove silently back to the farm.

The physician had given Minnie sedatives to take. Nellie brought her some water to swallow them with in her bedroom. Then she helped Minnie put on her night clothing and put her to bed.

It was a bad day.

The board of directors of the Farmers and Merchants Bank of Osceola met on August 5, 1907, and passed a resolution to honor Hardin's good life and honorable service to the bank and community.

Resolution of Respect

Resolutions passed by the board of directors of the Farmers and Merchants Bank of Osceola at its meeting held on the fifth day of August 1907, upon the death of Hardin R. Hammond.

Whereas since the last regular meeting of this board of directors, he—who does all things for the best—has seen fit to remove from our midst our dearly beloved friend, fellow member, and stockholder of the Farmers and Merchants Bank of Osceola, Hardin R. Hammond, and while it is hard for us to understand why such a good and useful life should be cut short so early, we realize that such is the way of this transitory life.

Therefore be it resolved that we, the board of directors of the Farmers and Merchants Bank of Osceola, ever found in our most worthy and esteemed member and associate an honest, faithful, prudent, and truthful man, who ever had the best interest of those for whom he was acting at heart; that he was a gentleman in the true sense of the word and possessed the highest type of manhood; that in his council, we gained much wisdom; that he was courageous and industrious, and that "Endeavor to do right" was his motto; that he will be greatly missed by us, his associates; that we now extend our heartfelt sympathy to his estimable family in this hour of bereavement and trust that they will follow the noble example set by their dearly beloved father and husband during his lifetime.

Be it further resolved that a copy of these resolutions be sent to the members of his family and that a copy be spread upon the records of the actions of the board of directors of the Farmers and Merchants Bank of Osceola.

Minnie

Minnie lay in bed for three days. She would not eat or drink. The pain of the sudden loss of Hardin combined with the responsibilities of the large family and farm shocked her being as no other event ever had.

Her favorite sister, Nellie High, stayed and tried talking with Minnie to console her, but all Minnie wanted to do was to close out the outside world and remove herself from all activity. Finally, on the third morning after the funeral, Minnie put on her clothes and came out of her bedroom. She was pale and drawn in the face and walked slowly into the kitchen.

Nellie and Miss Emmy were happy that Minnie was up and gave her some breakfast and water. Minnie picked at her breakfast and finally spoke to them in a weak voice.

"Thank you for taking care of things for me. I just couldn't get up and face everything. Nellie, I think that you can go home now. I appreciate all that you have done and will always love you for it. I need to be alone today. Miss Emmy, please watch the children. I am going back to Hardin's favorite place on Old Baldy in his honor, and I will be back for supper. Don't worry, I'm okay. I just want to think about Hardin and about my plans for the family in the future."

Nellie gave Minnie a long and affectionate hug, and with tears in her eyes, she called to J. Belt to hook up the buggy. He would take her to Osceola to the train, and she would go back home to Kansas City. She had done all that she could do for Minnie.

Minnie walked out the door and went down the road to the bridge over Cooper's Creek. After crossing the bridge, she turned up the trail that Hardin had taken so many times to the top of Old Baldy.

It was a two-mile walk on the path up the hill through the sparse scrub oaks and hickory trees. Minnie walked slowly, feeling the warm sun on her back as she climbed to the top of the hill.

At the top, Minnie looked down on the valley with the creek running through the low areas. It was a beautiful sight: green corn, light brown harvested wheat fields, and brown and green patches of pasture. The pastures were sprinkled with black and brown cattle munching on grass or leaves and slowly roaming the valley. Trees and grass lined Cooper's Creek and made a winding imprint upon the bottomland of the farm.

Minnie Hammond

Minnie saw Hardin's favorite log, and she chose to seat herself in the place where he had sat with her so many times before. It gave her the feeling of still being with Hardin to sit in the quiet beauty of the hill.

Minnie allowed her thoughts to travel wherever they wanted to go. She remembered the many happy times that she'd had with Hardin. She had so many good memories of the music and picnics, and she remembered the sound of his hearty laugh at something she had said. He would always be with her in that way. Sitting on his favorite log, she thought that wherever he was, he would know that she had dedicated this day to him. It gave her solace and strength to remember him and his love in this way.

Minnie thought of the children and the Pleasant Valley Farm. She wanted to do right by Hardin's five children. She knew that she was the executor of his